LUNA STATION
QUARTERLY

Issue 032 | December 2017

Editor-in-Chief

Jennifer Lyn Parsons

Assistant Editors

Tara Calaby • Wanda Evans • Cathrin Hagey
Dana Mele • Megan Patton
Danielle Perry • Iona Sharma

LUNA STATION PRESS
NEW JERSEY

First Paperback Edition December 2017

ISBN: 978-1-938697-91-3

Luna Station Quarterly publishes short fiction on March 1st, June 1st,
September 1st, and December 1st. For more information and submission
guidelines, please visit our website at lunastationquarterly.com

For Luna Station Press
Creative Director - Tara Quinn Lindsey
Editor-in-Chief & Founder - Jennifer Lyn Parsons

 LUNA STATION PRESS
576 Valley Road #197
Wayne, NJ 07470

www.lunastationpress.com

info@lunastationpress.com

CONTENTS

Editorial

Jennifer Lyn Parsons

A software engineer by trade, Jennifer is a life-long lover of story with a capital S. Her work has been seen in various magazines and she has published three books, with quite a few more in her back pocket. She counts Jim Jarmusch and Laura Ingalls Wilder as two of her biggest influences. Make of that what you will.

When not writing either code or fiction, she reads books and comics, and sometimes makes things out of wool or paper. She finds joy in making things, be they digital or analog.

Double down.

There are choices to be made. Everyone is starting to get tired about being angry all the time. Our energy has to be expended more carefully, many of us are starting to accept we're in this for the long haul now. The world is broken and fixing it is going to take a long time.

There are bright spots in the darkness, points of light that shine and give us hope. We're not done yet, by a long shot. As I write this, Hollywood is taking hit after hit as men are being accused of things so many of us knew they were doing all along without repercussion. Allegations of sexual misconduct, assault, and abuse in every walk of life are surfacing. I count myself far from surprised, having already watched GamerGate unfold and witnessed James Damore's infamous Google memo go viral within the tech community.

The good news is that as hard on the heart as these stories are, they're signs of change. Sometimes the wound must be reopened and the infection cleaned out before the balm can be applied and the healing can begin.

As this process continues, we here at LSQ hold to our sacred duty. Our new call to action? Double down.

Firstly, we support women authors as we've always done, but double down on that definition, this year we opened up more explicity to those who identify as women in some significant capacity. A tricky definition, but one we feel strongly, collectively, that is worth the work.

Secondly, I'm ecstatic that after a lengthy hiatus our amazing blog is back up and running. Doubling down? Oh yeah, that's where we have a whole team handling the operations and a collection of new writers to bring fresh perspectives into the fold. I can't wait for you to see the fruits of their labors. I'm humbled at the generosity of time and energy and creativity these women are putting into their work here.

Finally, double down on uplift. The world is full of negativity and anger. The stories we as women tell can be dark, we can ask the tough questions. Here at LSQ we try to keep that darkness in perspective and whenever possible, provide uplift. It is, as our Creative Director, Tara Lindsey, is always telling me, about where you shine the light. We shine the light on women, their achievements, their unique creativity.

Thank you for joining us for another amazing issue, for helping to keep the engines on burn as our station rumbles through the skies, and for supporting the talented, creative women-identified authors in this issue as we share their stories.

L S Q | 032

While it's Still Beating

Emma Grygotis

Emma Grygotis is a scientist and writer
from Rochester, NY. She is currently
pursuing a Ph.D. in Pharmacology and
working on her first novel.

The insurance packet had arrived months ago. They were hard to miss, the high-gloss oversized envelopes. The stylized blue heart and inset wrench in the lower right corner was always there to eliminate any final shred of hopeful doubt.

Hard to miss, so much color in an ash-gray apartment. Hard to hide. But Alice had tried nonetheless, burying it under the teetering pile of bills and partially-graded student exams that occupied their already small kitchen table. You could barely see anything in the smog-filtered light that made it through their nth story window anyway. Good enough.

Good enough, that is, until the morning Lenore gets up early, offers to make breakfast. Rehydrated egg whites, instant coffee. Again. Still, nice of her to offer.

But then Alice drags herself out of bed fifteen minutes later to find Lenore sitting in the kitchen, hands in her lap and fingers intertwined. Idle. Instead of the standard bowl of gelatinous white paste, a clean tabletop and an open envelope.

Mental note: throw it out next time.

"I'm going to do it," Lenore says.

Revision: burn it next time. Who would notice a little extra smoke?

"Please," Lenore asks. "Please just read it?"

"I know what it says."

It says the same thing insurance letters have always said. It says that you would never think of driving a car without keeping to a maintenance schedule. It says that oil must be changed every 3,000 miles, tires every 30,000. Parts go bad after all, especially the soft bits.

It says that the human body is no different.

Once, years ago, Alice could read Lenore's moods by her eyes. She'd never been able to hold eye contact comfortably. When confronted she would fall into a nervous, irregular rhythm, searching the room for a focal point, never settling. Even once Lenore's vision began to fail and she viewed the world through squinted eyelids and thick panes of glass, the reflexive darting motion had never stopped. Alice could still remember the way her eyes had once caught the light as they moved, flecks of amber against soft green.

Instead, two blinking red pinpoint lights. Clicking. Whirring with every incremental adjustment of the ocular replacements embedded within the eye sockets of Lenore's skull. A mechanical soundtrack that now accompanies their every waking moment.

Except now the red lasers are directed straight back at her.

Focused.

Unmoving.

Silent.

"You don't have to do it," Alice says. "You have a choice."

Lenore seems to think that is funny. Or at least, what passes for a laugh escapes around the standard-issue air filter embedded in her trachea.

"You really think so?" The cameras slowly rotate downward, gears grinding against one another before stuttering to a halt. "I've decided to do it."

Not again.

Again.

Someone should make coffee.

Alice finds herself in the kitchen, turning toward the sink, maneuvering a thick glass jar around a graveyard of dirty dishes into position below the faucet. The rusting pipes deliver water with a metallic scream.

She knows what it says.

It says that Lenore will enjoy a 33% median lifespan extension.

Reduced risk of myocardial infarction.

With less than 5% procedural mortality.

And if there was any doubt.

Exemption from age-dependent premium increases.

There's no way to heat the water, they ran out of the month's fuel ration three days ago. But she mixes in the powdered coffee crystals anyway, returns to the table still stirring, watching the clumps spin round and round, until one succumbs to the vortex and drops below the surface.

"I won't let them." Alice hopes she is at least convincing in her resolve, her entire weight pushing down on one slender wrist, bulging skin and thinning bone that, if you put any faith in statistics, should have snapped last year. The insurance company has said that too. More than once, reminding her with each successive price hike that she can exchange porous bone for medical-grade steel any time she chooses. That humanity is a luxury that she can no longer afford.

But it's the chair that snaps first, sending Alice careening head-first into the table and the jar tumbling into the air.

Then she's on the floor, staring up at the corrugated metal underbelly of their kitchen table. When Alice finally rights herself Lenore hasn't moved, still sitting with spine straight, palms pressed against her lap, a quiet resignation that Alice doesn't recognize. Then Lenore climbs down from the chair, settles in amongst the sopping paper and pooling coffee to press her face against Alice's shoulder.

"It's just a heart, Alice."

The dust settles, a new layer of grime accumulates. Their monthly premium is already far too high, and they both know why. There is nothing left to be said.

Certainly not, "thank you."

That would mean admitting it.

That night they lay together in the darkness, no longer listening to the beating of each other's hearts, but to the one that will soon be replaced.

The Smile

Irene Grazzini

Translator: Joyce Myerson

Irene Grazzini, a young native of
Arezzo, Italy, is a radiologist by day in
a Tuscan hospital. When not practicing
medicine, she finds herself inventing
both possible and impossible universes,
past, present, and future. Two recently
published novels of hers, (called
Dominant and Recessive, published by
Fanucci, Rome) have been acclaimed by
lovers of speculative fiction. The Smile
is her first publication in English. She
hopes that further forays into the North
American world of science fiction and
fantasy become a regular part of her
personal future.

You, who pass before me and gaze without seeing me, do not forsake me. Please stop. Help me, if you can. Or at least allow me to recount my sad fate, because there is nothing lonelier than having a memory which cannot be shared.

My name is Lisa. My name is one of the few things I have left. It endures, despite the ravages of time. Sometimes I would like to forget it and plunge into oblivion. It's better than plunging into madness. Consciousness is not a privilege. It is only the most perverse form of torture that God could have envisaged. No, no god could have wanted this. A demon, perhaps. Or perhaps only a man who wanted to be a god.

I remember the first time he set foot in my home. It was to be a joyous event, but it turned out to be the dawn of my ordeal. It was the occasion of the birth of my son Andrew, a pampered ball of fluff that attached himself to my breast, waved his little hands about, earning all the love from his wet-nurse and siblings. He was the second male that I had brought to light, and my husband, Francesco, decided to convene a solemn banquet to thank Our Lord for his benevolence.

I did not yet know that this benevolence would soon evaporate.

I had worn my best dress—two segments of velvet, inlaid with silver, and laterally tied with ribbons that exposed the white of my undergarment. The cuffs reached the fingertips at the back of my hand, and on the other side opened into a "V", beginning at the wrist, so as to leave my palm uncovered. The broad plunging neckline displayed the powdered skin of my chest.

I can almost hear again the sound of the strings and feel the rhythm of the dances. I have always loved to dance, as much as long skirts and a sense of propriety would allow. That evening I had much else to think about: upholding the honour of the household was entrusted to me, while my husband entertained the relatives and other guests. The scions of the most illustrious Florentine families had descended upon us in great numbers, enticed by the good food and especially the diversions that the banquet would offer. Francesco wished for it to be long-remembered, and had also invited all of the prominent personalities of Florence.

He among them.

He did it for me, my Francesco. He was fifteen years older than me, but he loved me. He could not have known that he was signing my life sentence. Or perhaps it was my own pride that condemned me. But the punishment has immensely outweighed the sin.

The table overflowed with wild game and select dishes. The wine did not linger long in the goblets, and immediately began to loosen the tongues of our fellow diners. It is with great effort that I try to remember its taste. It was like a sweet nectar caressing one's throat—an illicit pleasure, or maybe just an idealization of something that I can no longer have. My only prevailing taste is one of ashes.

Perhaps I drank too much that evening and the wine emboldened me and made me curious. "Curiosity killed the cat," my mother always told me, before consumption did away with her. I used to laugh and pretend to meow. It was a humorous game we played. Now I know she was right.

Not everyone ate and laughed under the light of the golden candelabras of our palace.

He stood apart from the jubilant throb of sounds and colours, his brow marked by a deep and definite frown line. Perhaps it was this that intrigued me, or the aura of energy and mystery that pulsated around him. Just looking at him you understood that the man's fame was justified. He was neither tall nor robust, but he stood out from his companions around the table like a flame among faint shadows.

Nearing that flame, we risked being burned.

I withdrew from the convivial humming of the hall and followed him onto the terrace overlooking the garden. The air was strangely hot considering the season, almost sultry. I rolled up my sleeves and moved forward towards the balustrade. The vegetation was a labyrinth of hedges and roses that disappeared into the dark of night.

Out of the corner of my eye, I studied this bizarre guest. He was wearing a dark surcoat above his tunic, well-made but certainly not as elegant as those worn by noblemen or wealthy merchants. It was worth less than a tenth of my dress. His hair and sideburns were streaked with grey and his thick beard gave him an almost scruffy look. He could not be described as handsome, but he had something that inspired awe.

"Messer Leonardo?" I tried to engage him.

The man jumped as if until that moment he had not noticed

me. He was leaning against the stone parapet staring into the darkness, his fingers entwined, his lips moving without a sound emerging from them. He turned to look at me. His grey eyes shone in the flare of the torches, as he studied me from head to toe.

"My Lady," he delivered these words —stiff and courteous—with a slight bow.

"I am pleased that you found the time to accept our invitation. I know that you are extremely busy in this period."

A hint of a smile on his lips, the first of the evening, and it was directed at me. I was charmed, I must admit. I was a fly, dancing in his spider's web.

"I am constantly travelling between Milan, Florence, and Rome. But I always try to carve out a moment for my studies. And for the celebrations of my fellow Florentines." He paused here to register my appreciation of the fact that he considered Florence his home. "And who knows, perhaps to find fresh inspiration."

I moved a step closer—as close as decorum would sanction. Those grey penetrating eyes absorbed all my attention, the banquet's din mere background noise. I had even forgotten about Andrew who was awaiting his next feeding. On the terrace, where light and dark were competing for dominance, there was no one but us.

"I have asked myself what inspires your paintings," I admitted. The master adjusted his garment over his shoulders.

"It matters not from where I start... merely what I seek."

"And what is it you seek, then?"

Leonardo lowered his voice conspiratorially.

"That which man has been seeking for centuries, my Lady, from the first dances around the fire to the experiments of the most learned: to fly beyond our limits. And the ultimate limit to conquer is time. Even the great alchemists of Antiquity, such as Hermes Trismegistus himself, were attempting to do this.

I had no idea of what he was speaking. My culture did not extend beyond housekeeping and singing. I barely knew how to read and write. But I nodded anyway. There was something intrinsically overpowering about this man's words.

"Only perfection can defeat time and become immortal."

"So you are seeking immortality?"

"You are a shrewd woman." Again that smile full of mystery. I felt my face grow red with heat, but I sensed a cold tingling down my spine. I paid no attention to it, so flattered was I by the great artist's compliment. "The ideal subject for a painting. I will be staying in Florence a while and, at the moment, I have no commissions. Would you permit me to place my art at your disposal?"

A painting by Leonardo would excite envy on the part of the other Florentine families who did not fail to remind Francesco of their noble birth, calling him "a wealthy but common merchant upstart." This would change their minds.

I nodded eagerly. "I would like a portrait."

***

I began posing for him the next day. My husband was as thrilled as I was at this unexpected opportunity. To tell you the truth, he was convinced that he had commissioned the portrait and that Leonardo had accepted. Why should I have shattered his illusion? He provided the artist with food and lodging in a dwelling in the vicinity of Palazzo Gondi. It belonged to our family and was close to Piazza della Signoria.

Every morning I left the house together with Catherine, my lady's maid, and so eager was I that I barely touched the cobblestones of my street, the Via della Stufa, as I hurried along. The wind carried the peal of the bells from the Cathedral of Santa Reparata and the scents from the shops of artisans—of leather and terracotta—but I paid no attention. I only thought about my coming encounter with Leonardo, about those eyes of his that seemed to read my soul, about his hands that travelled so swiftly over the panel creating something stunning from nothing. Initially he devoted his energies to the background. As I sat still, Leonardo breathed life into a landscape transformed by a continuous and nebulous mixing of the browns of the earth and the blues of the sky, without clouds, as the scene itself was all one endless cloud.

"This is the Arno River," he explained to me at the end of each sitting, "and here, between these rocky spurs and peaks, the road to Rome wends its way...."

However, after more than a month, he hadn't sketched in the human figure. One evening I tried to point that out.

"All in good time," he dismissed me with a curt gesture. In the last few days his good mood was evaporating and he was becoming nervous. I noticed that he was wearing a signet ring on his finger—a snake biting its own tail.

***

I was neglecting my children and my housework in order to pose for him. A strange frenzy had taken hold of me. I wanted that portrait to be finished, and also that it would be considered the most magnificent and realistic painting ever. Leonardo's enthu-siasm had infected me and at night I woke up soaked in sweat, thinking about that panel, which obsessed me more and more. I had lost my appetite and Francesco made me consult the best doctor in Florence, fearing that disease, which causes one to spew blood. The doctor found nothing and limited his advice to my imbibing an aromatic tisane.

I continued to dream of the painting in which my face had not yet appeared.

Leonardo's study filled up with new contraptions each and every day and his work became more feverish. He, too, got thin. The white filaments of his beard multiplied as if in a sudden snowfall. But even though his sunken eyes were circled in purple, they blazed out with a ferocious energy.

He started to scare me.

***

Work slowed. Leonardo had received another more prestigious and lucrative commission destined for the Palazzo Vecchio's Salone dei Cinquecento. He was not the type to care about money, and I'm sure that he would have continued to create even if he did not receive a single florin, but money served to buy paint and canvases.

So that he could seek his perfection.

He drew human figures and studied their anatomy. He designed strange devices that reminded me of birds. I remember all the sketches scattered on the floor of his room. Since they did not satisfy him, he walked all over them.

Catherine often refused to accompany me. She said that the

man was mad and begged me to give him up. I would have done it, had Leonardo not finally begun to work on the painting's focal point—me.

Only that woman was not really me. She personified the characteristics of virtuous women, with her right hand placed upon her left, her dark robes, and the black veil according to Spanish and Roman high fashion. She was a fascinating accomplished woman, who fully embodied the social aspirations of my husband.

"But it's fake!"

This was Leonardo's cry when the work was unsatisfactory. Then he tore up his drawings, flung his glass beakers all over the place, and only the sound of smashing covered the clamour of his cries of displeasure—the keening of a wild beast that had missed his prey by a hair's breadth.

The problem was the face.

First he tried putting a bonnet on my head. Then he opted for a veil.

"No, it's not right. It's not perfect. It has to be perfect!"

"Perfection rests only with Our Lord, who has created us in His image," I asserted one evening when bidding him farewell. I admit his eccentricities were beginning to irritate me. Leonardo stared at me and suddenly his face began to glow in a radiant blaze of light.

"My Lady, come back at the next new moon. We will then have what we both seek."

He was correct, unfortunately, but not in the way that I thought.

God forgive me, but my only crime was one of ignorance.

***

When I entered his study, the dust motes were dancing inside the sliver of light that filtered through the wooden shutter, partially-closed to keep out the rest of the world. His glass beakers twinkled ominously on the table. Time stood still. Leonardo was seated on a stool, his chin resting on the back of his hand. His gaze was intensely fixed on the finished panel.

It took my breath away.

I had seen many masterpieces. Florence, in this period, was a fiery forge of artistic invention, and my husband was a passionate lover of art, besides a silk merchant, but I had never laid eyes on such a marvel. It wasn't so much the hazy landscape, the accuracy of the ample low-cut garment, or the transparent veil entwined in the hair. It was the face, rendered with the softest of brushstrokes, so delicate as to make one doubt that they were the work of the hands of the man, whom I had seen shatter vases, and violently fling paint at the walls.

But this was Leonardo. Both gentle and violent. A genius and a madman.

"It's perfect," I murmured, fascinated by the smile that barely touched the lips of the face in the painting. Leonardo was fiddling with the serpent ring.

"But not real," he lowered his voice, "Not yet!"

I paid no attention. Ah, had I only understood the true sense of those words! Had I caught the gleam of lucid madness in his gaze! But it was not so. And I accepted the goblet that he extended towards me in order to toast the good outcome of the painting.

I realized my error too late.

I had to lean on the easel. My head was spinning. The scarf around my neck seemed heavier, and the air surged around me, quivering like molten lava.

"Poison," I thought in a flash of terror—a treachery that had ensnared many a nobleman in palace conspiracies. But why me? It did not make sense.

"It is not poison," Leonardo seemed to have intuited my thoughts. He was standing with arms crossed, concentrating his gaze on me with avid anticipation. He had not drunk of that liquid concocted in one of those mysterious glass beakers! I blinked rapidly but could no longer keep him in focus. Now everything rippled like water around me, the room whirling in a misty vortex, in which only the eyes of the artist—two shadowy cavities—and that snake remained constant. I thought I saw it move, as it eternally bit down on its tail.

The ouroboros.

The symbol of the disciples of alchemy.

Then I felt faint and the universe dissolved in a swirl of colour.

***

I would have preferred to stay stuck in that blinding rainbow. I would have preferred not to see. But I saw.

I saw myself standing in Leonardo's room. My clothes, my hair, my face. But it wasn't me. Something was missing. I struggled to find the word that epitomized that sensation.

She was missing humanity—that imperfection that makes everything truly real. Just as it had been absent in the woman painted in the picture...

When I understood, I tried to scream, but an indefinable smile remained glued to my lips. I tried to flee, but I had neither legs nor arms, except for those frozen onto the wood panel. I tried to close my eyes, but they would remain open forever.

I saw Leonardo place a hand on the shoulder of the Lisa that would exit that room to take my place in the world. She would hug my children to her bosom. She would warm the bed of my husband. She would live and die without ever having been born, only created by the hands and the magic of an artist who peered into secrets too profound.

The same magic that imprisoned me in a truly perfect painting, with its aura of mystery.

***

I have seen the sun rise and set too many times beyond this glass that separates me from the world. I have seen wars and diseases bear down on my people, the glory of kings and their fall in a bloody Revolution. I have been in sumptuous castles and in rooms behind a braided red cordon. I have been abducted and even pelted with acid and stones. But I am still here, and I ask myself what meaning can all of this have? In what way have I offended Our Lord to deserve such a fate? I loved my sisters and my brothers. I respected my parents. I was faithful to my husband. I gave birth to five splendid children. I lived a pious life, and attended mass in the Churches of Santo Spirito, Santa Trinita, and Santa Croce.

And my home no longer exists, my loved ones buried long ago. Only my name has remained.

Lisa.

It is the eternal echo of a grief that drives me mad, and leaves me encased in solitude, beneath the stares of strangers, as the seasons scroll by.

***

I cannot die. Oh, if you only knew how much I have desired it! I no longer feel hunger or thirst. I am a spectre without peace. The hourglass of time has stopped for me and in your eyes is reflected my timeless face, simulacrum of eternal damnation, touched by that enigmatic smile.

My fate bitterly mocks me. Not even weeping is granted me. Even though I feel stranded in enduring misery, I have to continue to smile.

As you scrutinize my smile, your eyes betray just how fascinated and frightened you are by my presence. I know that you feel it, even if you call it the mystery or magic of art. I know that in your most hidden unconscious, contemplating me moves you. You feel that my eyes follow you wherever you place yourselves in this room. They follow you, while you file before me in throngs on the other side of the red rope, and then with a vague sense of disquietude as you continue your visit. Centuries separate us as well as the glass of the protective casing, but we have walked on the same earth and experienced the same emotions.

Perhaps you would not have acted differently in my place.

O strangers from a world in constant flux, I only ask you this: Live for those who no longer have such fortune. Smile for real, in keeping with your deepest wishes. And remember Madonna Lisa Gherardini, wife of Francesco del Giocondo.

Or simply Mona Lisa.

Running Straight

E. K. Wagner

E. K. Wagner is an assistant professor within the SUNY system. She lives in the Catskills, inspired by Rip Van Winkle's game of nine-pins. Her speculative fiction has appeared in Apex, Perihelion, and Asymmetry, and her poetry has been published in the South Dakota Review. She is a member of SFWA, and you can follow her on Twitter @ek_wagner. Her website is https://erinkwagner.wordpress.com/.

When my madi had dreams, she had the best dreams—splashy, bold dreams with lots of color, and when she told her dreams to the story circle, those were the best nights, the nights I felt alive. "Careful, Cinti," she would say. "Be careful that you remember these." And I was. I hoarded the dreams in my head until I thought they might tumble free from my ears. I knew the dreams where she traveled straight through the hills like a ginger-rat seeking out the quiet places with dripping water where the roots sank deep into underground streams. "That's good water," my madi said. "Good water that will keep a girl like you going for many miles." Sometimes in those dreams, there were fearsome animals lurking in the weeds, watching the ginger-rat with yellow eyes. But the ginger-rat knew what she was doing. She crept through the grasses and if any striped cat snapped at her bushy tale, she hissed and kicked out with her back feet. And then she ran, and she ran swift as the river which ran outside our houses. "That was a river made by men," my madi said sometimes when she sat beating out our clothes on the rocks. "And that means it's flawed, Cinti. All man-made things, they have flaws." And then she would smile and she would tap a finger at her neck, just below the collar they made us wear. "They have flaws," she laughed.

In the hot years, we were worked hardest. And the hot years were longer than the cold. The sun in the hot years was close to us and seemed almost white out of the corner of my eye, it was that hot. I didn't have much schooling, not like madi, but even I knew that the fire burns hottest when it's white, the coals nestled together in the center of the pit were a lighter orange when the flames leaped high. The cold sun was a dark red and it sat low in the gray sky. I loved the cold years. In the cold years we didn't work so much because the fields were dead. They would send the girls and boys like me to lay traps then for small meat-animals, such as squirrels and prickle-backs, and that's what we'd eat.

They didn't let madi go beyond the fences or any of the other women. I knew when I turned sixteen years that they would collar me and keep me inside the fences too, and I was scared of that day. I liked too much running through the tall grasses and weaving out the strings of the traps and balancing them just so. I liked sitting on the hill just to the east of the fences and resting my chin on my hand so that the purple-budded flowers that still grew in the cold years tickled my nose. And I would stare down into the fences and see the fields stretching long away from me, past where I could see, dark and unplanted, and the houses where we lived clustered this side of them on the bank of the river. Outside the fences there was a bridge over the river and each night that I came back in from the traps, I would lift up a stone under which I had been keeping track of the days and make another mark. There were only eighty-one days in a cold year, and two hundred in a hot, and it took me some time to make sure my adding was right. But on one of the last days of the cold year, when the air had been growing gradually warmer and the red sun was smaller in the sky, I figured I had only two years left, a hot and a cold, and I would be collared like madi.

In the last of the cold year, madi was often low. She smiled less and muttered more under her breath. The itchin men watched us closely then. They walked by the houses more and whistled loudly at night so we would know they were there even when we couldn't see them. I had asked madi once why we called them that, the itchin men. "Because the itching after is almost worse than the whip," madi had said and she had been laughing then because we were in the deeps of the cold year when anything could make madi laugh, "when you're healing your body and your blood and skin are fighting back at them. And you itch. But itching means you're winning."

They didn't beat the women often, mostly because the collars did all their work for them. Madi was forced to wear it anytime the sun was up and she winced when the itchin men came even though she tried to hide it from me. They came, three at a time, one holding the collar out as if he were afraid to go near madi, the other two with black looks on their face and with their whips curled in their hands. They also had other weapons stuck in belts at their waists, heavy metal tubes with stubby handles. I had never seen one used and madi said they were worse than the whips because they didn't just hurt you, they killed you dead. The inside of the collar had needles thin as hairs that glinted like glass in the first rays of sunlight.

When I asked madi how she stood it and how the needles didn't make her scream, she said that pain could only hurt so much before you knew it like a friend. "And friends can only help us, Cinti," she whispered. But she was holding me close under the blankets and watching the night-sky growing light. "How can the collars help us?" I thought of the marks under the stone on the bridge. "They're hiding us, little," and she called me the way she had called me when I was young, stroking my hair. And then she held my fingers close between hers and I shivered because her hands were cold. She asked if I was dreaming yet and I told her that when I slept, I didn't see anything—no colors, no stories, no ginger-rats. "You, you're my ginger-rat, Cinti," she breathed into my ear, but I didn't understand and the itchin men came and they dragged me to one corner and I watched them put the collar on madi. She was thin and in the new light, a yellower light as the hot sun gained over the cold, I could see the white shift she wore pressed up against her ribs.

The women sat down in the story circle more during the hot sun years, and this is something I did miss in the cold years. The story circle was nothing much but a couple of stumps pounded into the ground and a pile of ashes in the middle where we built a fire over again each night. At night, when the sun had finally set, after we had eaten our share from the fields baked into bread or cooked into mush, madi and I joined the circle with the others, the girls like me sitting in front of the women. I leaned my head back against madi's knees and her long cotton skirts smelled a bit like the purple buds from the cold years when the fire warmed them.

The boys were never there and madi said that we were better for them not being there, but some of the women looked lonely without their children, especially if all they had were boys. "The boys leave us once they've grown," my madi said, and her face twisted when she spoke. "When are they grown?" She turned me and pressed me down on my knees so she could braid my hair while still sitting on the bed. It was better when in the fields to not have my hair long and getting in my eyes or, worse, getting caught in some of the machines. A girl had had her ear torn off a few years back because she had left her hair loose. "They're grown the same as you, Cinti," and madi let her voice drop low. And I knew she meant that the boys left when they turned sixteen. I didn't ask where they went, because I was afraid of where it might be.

The stories the women told were the dreams they had at night.

Even the itchin men came to hear them spin out the colors, standing stiff at the edge of the light where it turned suddenly to dark, and they seemed to listen close. The woman who lived in the house next to us always told dreams of boats. Boats came up the river, she said, boats with sails like ghosts, white and filmy and see-through. I didn't understand how such sails would catch the wind but I could see them when she described them. She didn't seem happy when she told her dreams, but she seemed settled and resigned. She had eyes like tear-drops, big and drooping, so it seemed like she was always sad and her lips didn't curve up when she smiled, so I always wondered if something had happened to her when she was little to make her so. Herri was older than most, even madi, and her pale skin was wrinkled like folds in paper. And she used her hands when she spoke, as if she were pushing the boats up the river herself. "Who's on the boats?" one of the little girls asked, one of the girls who still had to have a rope tied around her waist to keep her near her madi in the fields. "Spirits. Spirits on the boat, little. With wings gold like the grain at harvest. And they smile and they wave and they're coming to take some." Here, my madi tensed and she placed a hand on my head and I could feel her fingers digging deep through my hair to the scalp.

When madi told stories, there were no boats. It seemed that madi always told her stories last and the other women in the circle would lean slightly towards her when she talked. And madi spoke soft so that the crackle of the fire seemed a part of her stories, competing with the words. "Straight through the hills runs the red-badger," madi said, "not turning this way or that, but climbing over and running down deep, through the hollows. Where the trees bend down low, kissing the water, the red-badger drinks and she eats the roots of the lacy flowers. There's a snake slithering after and the red-badger, she waits in the grass, and she hears the snake pass. And just when the snake's almost

37

passed, the red-badger, she jumps and she bites as hard as she can. And she doesn't let go." And when madi said the last, she tapped my shoulder at every word.

The fields were longer than I could see the end of. Sometimes, at harvest, when the bag over my shoulder was full, madi would send me running back to the itchin men for a new one. Walking back to her, my bare feet cutting their own furrow, I stared out past the women and just watched the horizon. Once, when the white sun was burying into the dirt, I saw men on horses riding out of it, coming over the hills. I stopped where I was, and my madi looked back at me, her face tight. She waved her hand at me, telling me to come to her, but I couldn't move. The first horseman carried a white flag on a pole he balanced over his shoulder and it was almost see-through, the sun coming through it seemed whiter than ever. When they came closer, I could hear the horses' hooves on the packed grass at the edge of the field. I had only seen horses once before and they seemed too large for animals. Taller than me, I wondered how they could eat enough to not feel hungry.

The men who jumped down off the horses wore high riding boots, but other than that, they looked like itchin men, yellow braided collars and cuffs and buttons that shone almost too-bright. Our itchin men went to meet them, though some held back and walked slow, keeping an eye on us. "Here's a new one for you," the man with the flag spoke but he had handed it off to someone else behind him. "You can send your longest man home—Evert, I'm thinking?" The man had pulled a piece of paper from his pocket and was reading it for names. One of our itchin men smiled broad and dropped his whip as if he were leaving right that moment, jumping on one of the horses and running. He looked almost as excited as I think I would have looked to know that sixteen wasn't coming so fast and that I could still go outside the fences after this coming cold year.

A woman screamed. It wasn't madi, I knew, even before I looked at her. It was one of those who looked so lonely sitting in the story circle, her shawl wrapped high around her shoulders. She didn't seem to dream much, or she didn't tell many stories. Not anymore, at least, though it seemed I remembered her talking more when I was little. "Jonni!" She screamed the name and it was a name for children, like madi calling me Cinti when that wasn't my full name. She took off running for the itchin men even though we all knew that was craziness. The itchin men didn't like us to move too suddenly around them, and definitely not towards them. Herri was taking time to straighten, but she was standing near me, and she tried to grab the woman's shoulder as she stumbled past, pushing the stalks of the plants to either side before they whipped at her and cut her arms. "Baab, no," she said soft and then loud when the woman wasn't listening and threw herself off against Herri. Baab, like little, was something you called someone you loved and something you called someone when they were acting foolish.

A loud crack, like thunder, rolled over the fields and everyone grew really still. We all looked at the itchin men again, because we had been so distracted by the woman. The man with the paper was putting the weapon madi had told me about back in his belt. There was a young man behind him, if grown up, not too much. He had the look of an itchin man and was dressed as one, but he didn't have a whip yet and his face wasn't hard yet. He was the new one. His face was white and his lips trembling. Madi had still not moved and no one else had. Even Herri had been sure to keep her place when she was reaching out hands to stop the woman. The woman was on her back, not near anyone, the plants crushed under her, and she was staring up straight.

There was a hole in her stomach and blood. "In case you've forgotten," the man with the paper raised his voice and he had mustaches which fluttered when he talked, "we've got other kinds as can work these fields, we've got others who would gladly do what you do. The republic is merciful, but not unwaveringly so. Bury your dead tonight and double the yield tomorrow." And then he turned away to the other itchin men as if we weren't even there.

I had seen another burial, but I was young and I hadn't seen the woman die myself. The women wrapped Kila in blankets and they strung rope with rocks around her. We buried our dead in the river, madi said, because there they had some hope of seeing sunlight again, even if it did have to go through a lot of water. In a line, we all stood along the riverbank and with another, madi slipped her in. The current took her at the same time as the rocks, because the rush was strong here, so Kila moved as she sank, moved away from us. "May she see better things," Herri whispered. The itchin men were behind us and they seemed nervous, hands at their belts. When it was over and the sun was entirely gone, the itchin men came up to us and they took the collars from the women. Madi pursed her lips as the needles came out, touched with red.

We went to the story-circle afterwards even though we knew we would have to be up earlier than the sun tomorrow if we wanted to make our double-yield. The women were quiet for a long time and the fire had died low into red coals before anyone spoke. Finally, Puret told her story. "I dreamed this night that we all wore necklaces, but they were of the finest and softest gold and they did not choke us but lay gentle on our breasts." A hush settled on us and I looked at madi, confused. The itchin men didn't move and they didn't seem to hear, but Herri hissed, "Careful." Puret wasn't listening and her words were running and tripping into each other. "The fields were burning in my dreams and there was screaming, but we were laughing." Tears were welling up in her eyes but they didn't seem to fall on her face. "That's a long dream," Herri said, but, to me, it had seemed short. Herri didn't speak of boats that night. And when madi and I stripped down to our shifts and lay down in our beds, she rested her chin on my shoulder so she could talk into my ear. "That's where the boys go, little, and by the time they come back to us, they've forgotten they loved us. And so we have to forget we love them, the itchin men. And sometimes it's hard to forget." I wished very hard, my face pushed into the mattress beneath, that I could forget Kila screaming at her boy. "It's alright, Cinti," my madi said as if she could read my mind. "You don't have to forget everything just yet." I closed my eyes and didn't answer and tried to breathe like I was sleeping.

I woke up in the darkness and I wondered if madi had shaken me awake, but I could hear her breathing steady. My head hurt. I whispered to madi, close to her ear, "Madi, I saw something." I did not think she had woken up at first, but her breathing sped up. I could barely hear her when she finally answered, "Say it close to me, little," and I did. Then she sat up as well and climbed out from under the blankets. The room was already warming, because in the hot years, the heat was never really gone. Each house had only a few candles, but she took one up now and lighting it to fire with a match, she came back to the bed. She folded up the hem of the blanket and I saw she had sewn into the hem a series of stitches, all in a line. Madi had been counting too, because the stitches looked much the same as the marks I had made under the stone on the bridge. I felt cold, then, despite the warm air, and I grabbed madi's arm. "I have one more year." "You have as long as we can give you, Cinti," my madi said, and then "remember the dreams, little, always remember them."

The door opened and we had not even heard the steps of the

itchin men. They brought madi's collar because the sun would come up after we were already in the field. They have one for me too, I thought and started to quake inside, but they did not. It happened like it did every morning, me in the corner watching, and my madi standing straight and tall while the needles pierced her skin. For the first time, I thought my madi was beautiful, her red hair tumbling down her back and her green eyes that were sometimes gray flashing in the candlelight. I try to always remember her like that, but she does not visit my dreams.

After that night, I understood for the first time also that the dreams came with growing up, but madi said that the itchin men would not suspect unless I told them, not until I was sixteen years. And it seemed true, because I was allowed to go outside the fences when the cold year came. I missed the white sun more this year, though, and the red sun seemed to mock me. I thought of Kila and her blood. As much as possible, I worked alone, apart from the other girls and boys. I did not want to look out over the fields or the houses, because I worried what riders I might see against the red sun if the white sun had brought what it did. But I could not stay away from the eastern hill, so I crouched low in the grasses, huddling against the cold.

Sometimes, I fell into naps there, dangerous I knew, and when I woke, my fingers and toes would be numb. And I dreamed and it would always seem the same dream to me as the night I had woken my madi and she had counted the stitches. It was not a story like the women told. It was flashes and pictures and there was blood in my dreams. They would always end with my madi stepping out in front of me, between me and something I could not tell, and she would scream like I had never heard her scream before. I woke up sobbing. I shoved my face into my cold hands and tried to forget. But they began to come when I was awake too, growing up through the grasses, and sometimes, bent over the traps, I could not see the prickle-back, but only my own hands covered with red. I felt like the itchin men were looking at me differently when I came back into the fences.

My madi noticed it when I grew silent. She sat behind me, braiding and unbraiding my hair as if it was all she knew to comfort me. She asked me what I saw, but I would not tell her. "Cinti, you must tell me," she said when the sun was gone and her collar had been removed. We lay in the bed, nestled close to each other for warmth. She tried to tell me a story from the circle. "There is a little red sharp-toothed mouse in my dream," she whispered. "And it runs quicker than you can follow, weaving through the grasses, straight toward the hills." I told her that I did not want to hear about stories and dreams. "Cinti," and she sounded quiet, still as the grasses on a windless day, "they are not stories." I clutched the blanket closer and stared ahead into the black hollow of the room. I asked her what they were. "Our dreams are what will happen." Something caught in my throat and it felt like a sharp crust of bread, cutting me as I swallowed. "Madi," I said and I began to weep. She shushed me as if I were a small child, though she had not called me little since the night I had begun to dream. "Tell me what you have seen," she said again. I could not, even though I did not fully understand. Even though I did not really believe her.

"Will the collars make it stop?" My madi's breath drew in sharply. "The itchin men think it does. They're scared, Cinti, and they know it is the sunlight that lets us see, but they cannot keep us from dreaming. The dreams, though less clear, are no less real." The tears choked my throat as I tried to speak. "I don't want to see anything. I will go to the itchin men. I will ask for a collar." My madi's voice became stern and she sounded angry with me. "You must never do that," she said. "Why would you do that?" I thought of the dreams that came to me in the grasses.

"I am ordering you, Cinti, you must not ask for this." I told madi that I would not ask for a collar, but I did not sleep for the rest of the night. In the morning, the itchin men came and collared madi and she stared at me while they did it as if to warn me, as if to tell me with her eyes that I could not ask for such a thing.

The women told their stories in the cold year less often because the nights dropped to bitter temperatures. Even a fire banked high held only so much heat for us as we gathered near it. The itchin men stamped their feet at the edges of the light. Perhaps the red sun brought us fewer dreams, though it did not seem so for me. Even when my madi told her dreams and she whispered like the reeds around the stream in the valley and she chittered like the bald hare who nibbled at the leaves of the lacy flowers, I heard her screaming. "And the hare runs down the slope of the last mountain and sees ahead a water longer and wider than the fields. The water crashes at the sand and the dune-grasses. The hare knows there are ships here that will take her far away. Far away from the hawk." My madi's voice tickled at my ears and she tapped on my shoulder as she did every time she told her dreams. And even though she had told me now and I knew they were real dreams, they sounded less and less so to me.

I no longer picked up the stone on the bridge on my way back from the grasses to the fences. I did not make a mark for each day that passed. The snows came and covered the fields and the grasses in thick drifts, and the wind swept over it, kicking the flakes up into glittering funnels. Sometimes, I paused on the eastern hill and looked away from the fences and tracked with my eyes the prints left by some small animal running toward the other hills that crowded up close. "Cinti," my madi begged me each night, "tell me what you see." I would not tell her and I thought that perhaps this is why the itchin man brought collars each morning at sunrise to the women. If I told my madi that I saw her dying, that I saw her screaming and that I saw her like Kila on the ground, I was scared that the seeing might come true.

On the last day of the cold year, the itchin men built up large bonfires where they burned the last of the fuel stored against the red sun and its weak heat. They drank water boiled with fermented apples and hot spices. The women were not forced out of the houses to mend the fences and the boys and girls did not go out to tend to the traps. We had brought them in, with our last squirrels, and the itchin men let us keep our own catch on this day. Over the fires of the story-circle, the women spit the squirrels and let them roast. Fat dripped into the flames and the coals spat and sizzled. "Cinti, stay close," my madi said as she slipped the knife between hide and flesh, and the blade skissed through the tendons. I looked at her and then back at the fire. I saw her staring at me still out of the corner of my eye.

None of us saw how or when the bonfire spread to the roofs of the houses nearest the field. The red of the flames burned in our eyes and when I looked anywhere but at the fire, I could still see it dancing—against the dark sky, against the grasses, against the hills. The itchin men that had been circled around our own, though with relaxed stances, cups full in their hands, took a minute to register the roaring. Then they dropped their cups and the water splashed on the ground but that did nothing to stop the fire. Some yelled at us, ordering us to stay together and accusing us of spreading the fire, but most ran toward those houses that were spiraling into ash. "Cinti," my madi's voice was low and harsh in my ear. "Run, Cinti. Run." I turned to her, coughing, and my eyes were wet. "Madi, I can't leave." "Cinti," she held my face close to hers and she stroked my cheek and pushed the hair off my forehead. "Cinti, this is what I've seen. You must run." And she pushed me away. I stumbled, catching my feet under me, turning, running. Behind me, I heard the rough shout of one of the itchin men. "Stop!" But madi's voice was beating like a drum behind me, "Run, Cinti, run." I could hear the colors in her voice and like the ginger-rat and like the red-badger and like the sharp-toothed mouse, I ran. But I heard the sounds of my own dreams as well. The thunder rolled under the rumbling of the fire. My madi gasped like the sound a prickle-back made when the trap collapsed in on his leg. "Madi!" I turned and saw her falling. Herri reached a hand out towards me, palm up, stopping me. "Baab, go."

I stopped in the first hollow, farther than I'd ever been from the fields or the fences. I was crying and gasping. I was swallowing my own spit and choking on it. I had run straight to the hills and not turned to go one way or the other round them. Running up had been hard, but my legs had moved almost on their own and running down had taken no thought and little work. I could hear nothing but my own breathing and the whining in my throat. There was a creek ahead of me, choked by weeds, but, with the smoke and the pain in my throat, I did not stop to think, but dropped to my knees and scooped up the brown water in my cupped hands. It tasted of mud. A lace-flower brushed my ear as I lifted my head up, my hand still dripping over the creek, to hear back over my shoulder. My face stung in the cool breeze that still waited here in the shadows of the hills on the eve of the hot year. Crashing down through the grasses, an itchin man worked to stop himself at the bottom of the hill, his arms circling to find his balance. I didn't give him time to find it. Pushing myself up, I hurled my whole body at him, and he fell under me. I grabbed the killing weapon from his belt before he had caught his breath and I shoved it into his cheek. "You're just a girl," he said. And just when the snake's almost passed, the red-badger, she jumps and she bites as hard as she can. "That's not what my madi saw," I said back to him. And she didn't let go. I pulled the trigger and the weapon bucked crazily in my hand. I tumbled back off the itchin man. He spasmed, his legs and arms jerking, and then he went really still. I dropped the gun and I was still crying.

The white sun rose hot as I stumbled up the further hill. My chest and back hurt, and my lungs still wheezed with the tears in my eyes. My nose burned from snot and wet. I couldn't see the fields or the houses when I looked back but I could see the smoke fading out in the dawn sky. I couldn't see nothing but hills when I looked forward either, but madi had said to go straight.

Everybody and His Mother

Agrippina Domanski

I am a 20-year-old theology student.
My work has been published in The
Lampeter Review (The Bosnian War),
Current Accounts, Dumas de Demain
(in French, twice: La Guerre en Bosnie,
Rachelle), On Religion, and 34th
Parallel. One of my short stories has
won the Mearnes Award (The Truffle
Box) and another has placed among the
winners of the Audio Arcadia short story
competition (Marshes). Most recently,
my short story 'The Hairy Tooth' was
published in the Banbury magazine.

Auntie Diane's funeral had taken place on a rainy Tuesday at the Lawnswood Cemetery in Leeds. Sometimes people called Lawnswood "neo-Georgian", though it was really Victorian. But "Victorian" didn't seem specific enough. Auntie Diane had died on a Monday. On Tuesday, Jemima had stood at the cemetery all alone. Jack had left her all alone.

(Always protects the funeral, he does.)

God, what was she thinking? Always protects the kid, that's what she'd meant. Or maybe not. Maybe Jack was protecting the funeral from his presence. There was no reason for her to think that, but she did. Just like there was no reason why Jack wouldn't want to go with her, but he hadn't. He hadn't gone. And as always, the kid had copied him. Jack owned the kid's mind – and sometimes Jemima wondered if anyone else in the family deserved owning it.

Just a few hours before she'd been due to go to Lawnswood, Jemima had seen a dream. The kid had stood looking at the door of the house in London, where he'd never been, some distance from the well that wasn't there. Not really, not in Jermyn Street, thank God. But in the dream, there had been a well – a kind of lonely gaping hole in the green hair of the world.

Auntie Diane had been standing next to the well in Jemima's dream, looking very fragile with her bony legs sticking out of skinny jeans. The kid had thrown a stone at her (it had hit her head with a popping sound), and she'd fallen into the well head first. It was very similar to that horror film her sons had watched tonight. The Ring, that was it. She could now tell it had been inappropriate. Death was still too real in this house.

But back then, just a few hours ago, she hadn't had the guts to say it. Now she merely lay exhausted. What she had said and what she'd gotten back was enough. Jack must have bitten out a part of her heart.

At least she'd had the guts to ask Jack why he hadn't let the kid attend. (She'd only brought herself to do it two weeks after the funeral, and even this had felt like an enormous effort.) He could have at least said goodbye to Auntie Diane, right? That's what she'd said to Jack, or so she thought.

She'd hoped to talk to him alone, but when she'd come back home from the Amnesty International office (she worked as a charity fundraiser), she'd found him watching that Ring thing with the kid. And once she'd seen the kid tucked in under Jack's slender arm (it had covered him like a broad wing of a bird of prey), she'd no longer been able to control herself. This jealousy was some vicious circle she and Jack were forever stuck in: an emotional custody battle Jack was winning. The kid looked so safe, so calm, so happy around Jack – the way he never did when he was with her. Impulsively, she'd asked him:

"Are you sorry Auntie's dead?"

The kid hadn't had the time to answer. Jack had looked up at her in his cool, resentful manner, and muttered:

"Lay off him for fuck's sake, he's had enough of this shit."

"What shit? What you've got on the screen – that's what I call shit. And this is life, Jack. Death, it... it's a part of life, and –"

"Lay off him, I said. And no, it ain't really, not for normal folks." He'd swung his long legs down like a pendulum, catapulting himself upwards. "We're off. Come on kid, we'll go on a ride." Looking at her, he'd added spitefully: "Got my pay cheque today."

They'd only just left, it seemed. Or maybe an hour had gone by. Jemima still had their sickening movie playing with her nerves, but maybe it was endless. She pressed the power button on the remote without ejecting the DVD and let her head fall back onto the couch.

The sitting room felt big and empty, like a cold ocean. It seemed the entire funeral had taken place here, though of course it hadn't. But Jemima's mind had darkened from the pain, that peculiar heart pain any fight with Jack left her with – it accumulated, like the after-effects of angina.

She couldn't stand being in this room with the boys away. It seemed Auntie Diane's body had lain on the very couch on which she was lying now. "This here couch," Auntie had called it, or even "'ere", which sounded just like "her" pronounced in the North Eastern dialect. It was plain snobbishness on her part, aimed to show that try as Jemima might, Leeds wasn't London.

She hadn't stayed here long. Not in Leeds. Jemima had done all she could, but it was what they said about old people: they couldn't be moved around. Not even if everything had been done for their comfort.

The dark wardrobe in the moist and dusty corner at which she was unconsciously staring gave a low creak. The wind, it must have been, or maybe the boys had forgotten to close the door. It wasn't like Jack, but whatever. The funeral and the death spirit must have affected him, though he didn't show it.

She was very cold. It seemed to her that the wardrobe door was open, but she couldn't see (darkness was descending rapidly, like a carnivorous bird on a hunt – a raven, maybe). Auntie's wardrobe was watching her, the black gap she'd seen or imagined in it smiling at her like a crooked vertical mouth of some monster, or a slopping open wound. The whole thing was so rusty and shapeless it could well be a Scandinavian troll masquerading as a harmless piece of furniture. It was an enormous wardrobe, like in those Narnia novels.

Only it was neither magical nor harmless. She knew this much. This wardrobe hosted remains. The remainders of late Aunt Diane's life.

The house in which Jemima lived was a very big, empty house (there was hardly any furniture), full of cracks and draughts, but not yet haunted. No one had died there, from what she knew. Even Auntie Diane hadn't; she'd died in the hospital, in that shitty East Park Medical Centre with no one to hold her hand... And if anything, Jemima could bet Auntie had always wanted to die next to that bloody Gothic wardrobe. That's why she'd had it dragged in all the way from London and paid a fortune for it.

When they'd been taking Auntie away and making such a fuss about it, Jemima had already known at the back of her mind that Auntie wouldn't come back. Or maybe she hadn't known. It was hard to tell now. People always granted events with retrospective significance, as John Banville or some other self-proclaimed Irish philosopher had said.

She killed the lights and lay smoking in the dark, propped up on her elbows a little. They were going sore, but she didn't mind. The cigarette rested an inch away from the wall. She wasn't afraid to set the house on fire, even though the padding was inflammable. The house was too wet, and she had no energy left. If it burnt – well then, let it burn... Let her burn too, burn here in the dark... She wasn't worth much if her sons had turned away from her so easily.

She could see a kind of pale electric green gleam coming from the newfangled skyscraper round the corner. The glowing cigarette seemed to keep her warm, though nothing could stifle the cold coming up her windpipes from her diaphragm. She seemed to be breathing liquid ice, like a dragon that'd been fed a fire extinguisher. Mississippi Burning was a film that had scared the crap out of her as a kid, but how was it different from her life now? Jemima Preparing to Burn in Leeds... But that wasn't a catchy title.

Some headlights flashed in the window. She thought by association that killing the lights had been exactly what she'd done. Disconnected them from their life source.

(They'll want something to eat, now that they're back .)

She wondered if they'd find the pancakes she'd left them – and then realized Jack must have fed the kid elsewhere. He possessed a remarkable combination of teenage callousness towards her, and fatherly concern when it came to the kid. Somehow that insulted her most. If Jack found that job in the police force he wanted (she'd run into him reading the police force training manual a few times already), he'd take the kid away from her and the kid would readily go.

She knew why he felt that way. She wouldn't even go to court after Jack if he really did this, as she anticipated. The kid didn't like it that mum was always sad. And who could blame him? Jack was always so cool with his boiling dark humour – even Jemima admired this attitude. What scared her was that they wanted to keep chilling, even though the house was in mourning. They wanted to scare death away.

Taking no notice of her.

On a subconscious level, she knew what Jack thought of her. He was her son, after all – and for years she'd been his sole parent. He thought she was playing the saint now, even though she'd hated Auntie Diane herself. He had a point. It was hypocritical. Jack nearly always had a point.

For years, Jemima had tried to do right by Auntie Diane, whatever that was supposed to mean. But she'd mainly wanted to do that to feel her superiority. Her three-decades-long grudge against Auntie Diane had always been fuelled by a sense of righteousness, a sense that she treated Auntie better than she'd treated Jemima...

Of course, that in itself was an insult: a calculated insult Jack had made her conscious of. Jemima was busy with the saintly shit, not Peggy. Not Peggy her cousin, a famous and happily married Asian languages specialist who lived in the States now, in a nice big house in Louisiana, if one was to believe The New Yorker. Not Peggy, who'd left Auntie to rot in hell so help her God.

Peggy couldn't give a damn. That was the worst thing about it all. Jemima couldn't help giving a damn, couldn't help caring and turning the other cheek... And that's why she had two full-grown Peggies in masculine form lurking around her house now. Peggies who couldn't give a damn either – and who'd probably do much better than their mother in the end. That's what she'd learnt on her own skin.

Even in '85, when Jemima and Peggy had both been kids visiting Auntie Diane in London, Peggy had it all. Wherever she was, Peggy came with her empty palms turned upwards, as if in prayer, and her fluffy eyes wide open – and she always left with her pockets full. She'd even gotten the scholarship to study in the US after citing "extreme poverty". "Extreme poverty", bloody hell. Jemima knew Peggy was very good at showcasing "extreme poverty" – indeed, at acting as if she was poverty personified. It had always paid off for Peggy – just like it used to with Jemima's sweets.

Summer '85, yes, she remembered it well. Showers pouring non-stop over London, as if God had delivered a personal deluge over the city. They'd all pretended to be religious then. The Thatcher fashion had demanded it. Jemima knew it as someone with a sociology degree. And because no one had known how long the deluge was going to last, Jemima's parents had sent plenty of treats with her to Auntie Diane: French cheese they could barely afford, fresh rabbit meat and pots of home-made clotted cream from the Devonshire farm near their house.

Auntie Diane was – had been, Jemima corrected herself grimly – her mother's sister. Another sister had been Peggy's mother, killed by meningitis in the '70s when Peggy had been a toddler. Auntie Diane had been childless, so she used to invite Peggy over to spend holidays at her house. But not Jemima. She'd never been enthusiastic about Jemima, but God, she used to love l'il Peggy.

Auntie would unwrap all Jemima's treats and look at everything at once, like a capricious customer at the counter. Then she'd say she was allergic to this and that, and that none of it was any good at all. She'd always expressed her dissatisfaction to Jemima, as her parents' representative.

Once the presents had been unwrapped and sneered at, Aunt Diane would tell Jemima to take a walk. She hadn't cared about a lone child's safety, as long as the child was Jemima. The London of the '80s had been safer than it was now, but still not safe enough. But Jemima hadn't learnt that until much later. She used to always take that walk, like a good girl.

And once she'd left, Auntie Diane would lock the doors and draw the curtains down. Then, she'd cook all Jemima's treats for Peggy – and Peggy would eat them all and lick her lips. There would never be anything left for Jemima to try. She could tell now it was ironic. At home, her parents used to tell her this kind of fancy food was too expensive.

If she could be cynical, like Jack (but she couldn't), she'd have said Peggy and Auntie Diane had started a jolly good business of feeding off her, the soft-hearted idiot. Peggy continued profiting off that business streak of hers in Louisiana. And once Peggy had been safe in the States, Auntie Diane had carried on feeding and feeding on Jemima's mind, like a maggot squirming around its valleys.

She'd been happy to move to Jemima's house to be cared for, even though she'd already signed off all the money to Peggy. She'd even dragged her huge and inconvenient demonic wardrobe over, and Jemima hadn't had the guts to resist. Oh, she never had the guts to resist.

She couldn't even resist her own feelings. No matter how unfairly Aunt Diane had treated her, Jemima had always longed for her affection. That's why she'd taken her in the moment Auntie Diane had fallen ill. Not that this had been a good idea. The moment Jemima had arranged for the wardrobe to be transported to Leeds, Aunt Diane had secretly sold the London house to new owners. She'd sent the money to Peggy over the Atlantic, purely out of spite for Jemima.

And still Jemima had felt insulted on Aunt Diane's behalf, when the boys had skipped the funeral. Skipped it as if it was some boring Sunday service at a local church. Only now that Auntie had died, Jemima had seen what a weak person she was. She couldn't even discipline Jack. God, he was so strong. So ruthless.

In the dark nucleus of her mind it was obvious why she resented Jack's obsession with the kid so much. She had been the unloved child, the hated good-girl niece. She'd been the one endlessly exploited and ridiculed, and yet the one to always come back for more like some deranged, pathetic masochist.

As if one emotional beating hadn't been enough. She could still feel the blows on her heart. Even her parents hadn't treated her to things like Auntie Diane had treated Peggy. Even her parents hadn't fussed about her like Jack fussed over the kid.

She could hear the boys getting back in. It had to be after midnight. The scratch of the key in the keyhole made her shudder. (Jack always unlocked the door as if he was practicing for a break-in. Maybe he was. God only knew what his plans really were.).

The headlight beam she'd just seen must have been theirs. It meant Jack had taken the Toyota, ancient but powerful, was old girl... Well, well. She knew it got him off in a way, acting like the kid's surrogate father. She couldn't deny he was doing well. And there hadn't been a scratch on the kid's face for months, not even from a fall. In fact he was painfully happy around Jack – painfully for Jemima.

Jack was so strong, so young – he could afford to smile all the time, to ignore Auntie Diane's death, to go clubbing till dawn after a nine-hour shift. Jack was like some immortal beast brought down to Earth to shame his mother.

No wonder the kid felt nothing for her but a sort of condescending sympathy. How could she compete? She was mourning a death. She was too tired, too lifeless. No better than Auntie Diane. Maybe she was mourning her own death as a mother.

She really wanted to save this cigarette. She liked the stubs, and hated the fresh long white ones. Those looked like bloodless human fingers stuck in the doorway. But she didn't want either of them to see she was awake. Especially Jack. He would resent it all – all this sluggish sentimental snot.

Maybe Jemima hadn't loved Auntie Diane the person. But she'd loved the auntie who was part of her past, her childhood. Had been, not was. All of these things were had beens.

Jemima drew the blanket around her shoulders. She lay looking at Auntie Diane's wardrobe. It was a survivor, that wardrobe. The rest of the stuff had been passed over to new owners.

But this was the most important wardrobe. It hosted Auntie Diane's secret. Back in the '8os little Jemima used to think Auntie was a "Hair Krishna" (which she'd thought was a sort of creepy hairy rodent). Later on, teenage Jemima had thought Auntie Diane was a voodoo witch, and that she cursed people using all the hair – that the hair came to strangle the cursed when they went to sleep. Maybe Auntie had cursed Jemima's sons, who hated her... They'd hated Auntie's presence here, too, in what they saw as their territory. Especially Jack.

Jack would be able to afford his own place soon, she knew – a tiny place, but habitable. But he thought this Leeds house was the kid's territory. He was ready to protect the kid's interests with his teeth.

She remembered that Jack had just come home. A strong man and a worthless son. His presence was making her afraid.

She closed her eyes and hid her joint under the cone made of her pale shaking fingers, praying that they passed by without seeing she was awake, and that the turbulence didn't extinguish the cigarette stub. It could seem she'd folded her hands like that in order to pray properly, even though she'd never prayed. But now she did. She prayed that they left her in peace. Left her to rest in peace like Auntie Diane.

She'd known straight away Jack was bringing in a girl. There was a soft perfume smell in the air. Now they were trying to smuggle her into the bedroom, though Jemima could tell he'd been counting on making out with her here in the sitting room, where there was more space. It was disgusting that he'd do that a week after a funeral, that he'd want to fuck someone on this dirty sofa bed where Jemima was now pretending to be asleep.

The girl giggled – Jemima heard Jack promise her lots of booze once they got to his room. Now she could hear the kid rumbling about in the kitchen. She'd been calling Steve that for years, as if he didn't have a name. But he never answered to "Steve" when she called. Jack had been the one who'd started to call him "kid". And now he'd taken that as his name.

Slowly, she took her cigarette out from under her improvised lighthouse. It lit a small red circle around her face, as if she was a parody of an angel.

She didn't resent Jack for dragging the girl in per se. He had his hormones, he had the kid to teach how to do it all... And then

59

God knew he paid for it all himself from what he got off his service jobs. Jack always paid his way through. The rest was none of her business.

Her cigarette going dimmer and dimmer, she lay shuddering in her diminishing self-made circle of light. No matter what she did it wasn't warm enough.

That was why she didn't see Auntie Diane coming straight away . The light was moving in jittery jumps all the time, and she didn't notice the movement near the door, in the corner opposite the wardrobe. Auntie Diane didn't materialize, as ghosts were supposed to do – she didn't emerge as a shimmering presence in the dark. She didn't emit cold. In fact she emitted a kind of warmth in the frosted room – a heavy, nauseating warmth of a parasite-infested body.

The first thing Jemima noticed was Auntie Diane's physicality. She was wearing the dress she'd been buried in. But she didn't feel dead and she didn't smell dead. She didn't even look dead. That's why Jemima should have thought then she wasn't dead, but she was. Jemima had seen her face in the coffin less than three weeks ago.

The ritualistic time period for the soul to leave its past abode was forty days, from what Jemima had read in esoteric literature. And it hadn't been forty days – not even close. She couldn't even make use of this information.

Auntie hadn't died in this house. It was important to remember. But Jemima thought a soul belonged where it had felt in place, at home. Even so, however – Auntie hadn't liked Leeds any more than her own house in London. In fact she'd hated it. It all seemed very illogical – but Jemima had always thought humans tried to make the world more logical than it really was.

But when Auntie's ghost moved in the direction of the wardrobe, Jemima thought with a heavy, nauseous kind of understanding she knew what this was about – knew what Auntie wanted. Knew what was in that wardrobe.

She was convinced the Auntie Diane she was seeing wasn't really a ghost, but a biofield. Her late husband would have said so too. This light interest in all things occult had been part of what had brought them together as students. One of the creepiest punk things Jemima and her beloved had stumbled on were the writings of Jasmuheen, a New Age mystic. About biofields, Jasmuheen wrote that it didn't matter how many days had gone by, or where one's soul felt in place – this kind of thing was just a relic from the ghostly, long-buried Christian culture.

What mattered was the interaction between biofields. There was some kind of interaction between Auntie's biofield and the wardrobe in the dark corner: between her and its contents.

Jemima had never forgotten what lay in the first drawer just above the ground. What had lain there for years, absorbing the icy drafts of wind rising from between the floor tiles of the house in Jermyn Street – and from the very different cracked airways of this old house in Leeds. She couldn't forget. When she'd accidentally found it, it had scarred her eleven-year-old self too much.

Auntie's biofield had come for her hair. The ancient, curled-up buns of hair she'd saved up. They were full of stale, white dust that looked like powder; no one had touched them for decades, except for their aging owner. Jemima had thought of all this hair when she'd stood at Lawnswood all alone. Thought that she'd have to clear it out somehow, since Auntie had dragged the wardrobe over from London. Maybe it really was haunted and inescapable – and it inescapably haunted Jemima.

She'd seen those thick grey balls of hair as a child, packed in the drawer and covered with dust. There'd been plenty, but little Jemima had never had the strength to pull out the drawer far enough and look at them all (Jack would have done it in an instant). Now it didn't matter. The grown-up Jemima would have to clear the entire wardrobe and dispose of it all.

Their family wasn't Jewish, even though Jemima's husband had been, so there wasn't any ritualistic obsession with cleanliness. She wasn't disgusted by the hair either. But she knew it couldn't be left lying around – and it couldn't be thrown away. This was just as confusing as all the superstition stuff. Despite her Amnesty job, taken up to feed her children, in her heart she was a failed sociologist, like the rest of her family. She still had all the James Frazer volumes, including The Golden Bough, lying around in the kitchen. He'd written somewhere that a sympathetic connection existed between the hair and its owner. It was always safer to dispose of it after a death.

These soft, slowly decaying hair balls were like grey cotton threads cats played with, only they were thinner. It was all right here, yes. All the hair Auntie Diane had ever cut off. Faded, silver and seemingly hard and thin at the same time, to the overemotional Jemima they looked like metallic threads. Or the threads of fate woven and ruthlessly cut by the Moirae.

Only Auntie Diane hadn't wanted to cut hers. She'd keep her hair, her lifeline, preserved safe in the intimate darkness and hidden from sight, rolled up in balls, so that they were indistinguishable, inseparable from one another. By keeping all her hair, she'd hoped to prevent her lifeline from tearing, from ever being cut. And guess what, boys and girls, Jemima thought, drowning in muted shock that rang in her ears like a gong, guess what. It had worked; she was back. She'd attained her immortality. Now she wanted to make sure she'd have it forever.

Aunt Diane truly was a biofield, not a ghost; she had a physical body. It was a hot body full of energy, though this energy wasn't of the ordinary kind. Maybe it had come from Auntie Diane's hair, like Rapunzel's. That's why she'd come for it; she'd come to take her hair away into her grave.

Her biofield now hovered just above the ground in front of the wardrobe. She didn't emit a white glow like a ghost probably would. Instead, she still radiated heat. Jemima could almost see its waves rising from under her feet to the top of the room, like waters splitting to let a saint through. Jemima could see Auntie's face and her piercing profile with a long hooked nose and hard aquiline eyes. They had always been blue, but now they had a dark red glow. It could have been from Jemima's cigarette, but it wasn't; that had long since died out. Her numb fingers had split it in halves.

Auntie Diane looked at the wardrobe – Jemima could see the red dots in her pupils turn towards it – and its doors opened. There wasn't any noise, not even a creak, though that was unnatural. Jemima's ears had become blocked, as if she was travelling at a great height. She tried swallowing and couldn't do it.

The hair drawer crawled out once Auntie Diane looked at it, making Jemima think of a crab. She felt the surge of mind-eating terror. Auntie wasn't hovering. She stood completely still in the sickeningly warm air (it kept moving around her, as if rising to the top of a forest bonfire), as if it was a pedestal. And as she looked inside the wardrobe harder with her unseeing glowing eyes, the hair balls slowly started to levitate.

They rose into the air above the drawer and slowly floated out, following one another in a pattern resembling a loose scatter graph. Some thin single hairs must have been ruffled by the turbulence. Jemima could see them in the moonlight and the green glow coming from the skyscraper, now that the balls had shifted away from the dark corner. Now they were lit up with a green light.

Auntie Diane's biofield turned around, and floated slowly towards the window, followed by the balls behind and on either side of her. She looked as if she was leading a liturgical candle procession during the Easter service – though of course this was a blasphemous thought.

Jemima thought of the rock 'n' roll song she and Peggy had been brought up on: "Great Balls of Fire". But the fire had been in Auntie's eyes.

Auntie Diane and her procession travelled out of the window and into the monochromic moonlit sky.

Jemima half-sat in silence and perfectly still, staring at the window blankly, her elbows forgotten. With some distant part of her mind, she could hear shuffling and soft voices coming from Jack's room. Then the jingling of some jewellery. Jack's voice: "I'll call you tomorrow." She wondered if he was lying to the girl, and decided he probably was. Jack was no romantic.

She didn't look up or glance around. Instead, she listened to the sounds of Jack walking to the door to see his companion out. The kid was probably asleep by now. It was for the best.

As Jack stepped back into the sitting room, Jemima reached out and turned the light on with one sharp movement. He stared at her silently, in grim anticipation.

She licked her lips, and asked:

"Did you have a nice evening?"

"Yeah. I'm sorry we woke you up," he said flatly. She was sure he was. It meant he had to talk to her now.

She licked her lips again, and forced herself to say what she'd meant to say all along.

"I just wanted to tell you – you were right not to go to the funeral. You were right not to let him go, too. She was a witch, a real witch. And I've always been a coward."

Her son stared in astonishment.

It suddenly crossed her mind she could be a witch herself.

Just Like You

Elizabeth Martin

Elizabeth Martin writes short stories and longer works of fiction, always with a speculative element. She has taken writing workshops taught by Rebecca Makkai, Bess Winter, Rebecca Rukeyser, Steve Trumpeter and others. Elizabeth holds a Bachelor of Fine Arts from the School of the Art Institute of Chicago and a Masters in Library Science from Dominican University.

Their marriage had withstood the test of time. They were five years in, and in that five years they'd traveled, attained promotions and purchased a few extras they never thought they could afford. This was enough for five years and then it wasn't. So on her thirtieth birthday celebration, sometime between appetizers and dessert, they concluded it was time to start a family.

They went about it in the usual fashion. They read books, talked about parenthood with other expectant couples. Those going through it for the first time spoke of the love that brought them to this sacred place. Those going through it for the second or third time told them horror stories, but the horror stories always ended with the couple saying they wouldn't have it any other way. They babysat overnight for his brother and sister-in-law, a touch and go experience, but they managed. After all these activities, they registered, and in a few weeks a letter came with their appointment and further instructions for what they must do to prepare for their visit to the Barn.

The letter thrilled and terrified them. Their decision had suddenly become real and real anxieties arose. Would they be good parents? Would they have enough time, energy and resources to give a new being all that he or she needed? Would they satisfy the biological, neurological and physiological testing of the

Barn's strict protocols. And one more question arose, an enjoyable one, one that ramped up their anticipation. What kind of choices would they get in the creation of their unique being? The Husband couldn't help wanting a boy and maybe it might be nice if he—or she, for it could be a she—took after him in some way, in looks or in skills. A leaning towards engineering might be nice. The Wife stated that she didn't care about those things, and girl or boy, she just wanted their child to be healthy, but privately she admitted there were some features she preferred. They filled out the survey and sent it back in. The Barn would consider their answers but must follow the protocols established by the Universal Species Distribution Accord.

The drive to the Barn took two hours, hours which the couple passed with their lips pressed tightly against all the questions that could not be answered. Was it enough to have done what they had to prepare? Or was it a hollow exercise meant to artificially bolster their failing confidence? Somewhere along the journey, they both came to the same unspoken conclusion. They did not know what they were doing and had no business pursuing the course of action to which they now hurtled.

The transition from congested city to glorious countryside passed unremarked upon, but had a calming effect. The beauty of pasture land was something neither had ever experienced in life, though they had seen this type of sprawling nature in books, swaths of flowers and waving wheat, the dazzlingly blue skies and the chubby puffs of clouds. It was as though they were a real living part of the images in the government moving picture archives.

The Barn itself looked like an ordinary barn of the type used long ago, a reassuring presence and a symbol of bounteous fecundity. It was made of simulated wood planks painted red. Two windows, framed in white, almost touched the roof. The door was an open mouth below the two windows which functioned as eyes in a surprised but delighted face. How nice to see you! We are glad that you are here!

Inside there was nothing of the Barn's homey welcome. Row after row of glass petri dishes rested in steel trays which rotated to ensure optimal ultraviolet exposure from the brilliant circles of light overhead. Big Xs broke up the smooth tiles on the floor, drainage vents to catch the run-off from the sprinkler system. This was the nursery, explained the staff member who met them at the door, which turned out not to actually be open to the untamed elements, but covered with a thick felt-like material for filtering out impurities.

Not wanting the staff at the Barn to easily discern the shameful truth of their unsuitability, they did their best to present a cheerful confidence they did not feel. They smiled when they shook hands with the white-coated doctors, adopted a posture of nonchalance when these same doctors waved wands up and down their bodies, telling them to turn this way and that, to raise an arm or spread out a leg as the wands passed over and under, intimately checking for defects. Remarkably, they passed.

In the small consultation room, the Wife asked, "When will we know ours is ready?"

"Whoa now," said the Doctor in a folksy, friendly tone. "There's a lot that happens first before we get to that. This is just the initial evaluation." He smiled at the couple. It was not a scold. He had dealt with many excitable bonded pairs who had asked this very same question.

"Who gets to decide on the type of offspring, you or us?" asked the Husband.

"As was explained in the introductory literature, it is a mutually beneficial and equitable process free of prejudice. We can't have too many beings with a certain quality or ability, just as we can't have too few. And of course, we must allow for the occasional evolutionary surprise. We are a research facility as well as a reproductive clinic. The fact that you are here means that you have agreed to all parameters." He said this in a less folksy tone. The Wife gave the Husband a pleading look and after that he did not ask any more questions that could be interpreted as aggressive.

They were then led off in separate directions for the next series of examinations. First, a stress test involving various gym-like equipment done with electrodes placed on chest, arms and legs. It was very similar to a workout except for the zaps that came through the electrodes. The next test involved chemicals. Liquids sprayed unpredictably upon their face beginning with water and progressing to something which, although not toxic, had a foul fragrance. Finally, a chemical which produced a sensation akin to being sunburned was sprayed all over their bodies. This was for testing their ability to withstand the painful emotional turmoil involved in caring for an infant. The last examination had them running through an obstacle course meant to simulate the endurance it would take to raise the youngling through to adulthood.

But they withstood it all and eventually were brought back into two separate sterile rooms. Dressed only in a transparent sheath, each lay on a flat surface situated in the center of the room. At the command of the sterile garbed doctors visible behind protective glass, instruments came out of openings in the wall. Both the Husband and Wife had been sedated. They hardly noticed when a robotic arm with a rotating pincer whirred menacingly forward to grab a piece of skin. Another robotic arm moved in to slice off the upraised flesh and, almost immediately, a third arm was on the scene to staple and bandage. The whole procedure, after all the rigorous testing beforehand, took less than a minute.

Dressed and seated side-by-side in the doctor's office, they were again presented with forms. These forms provided extra insurance for the doctors, surgeons and attendants. They would not be held responsible should there be a failure to grow or if the growing in any way exceeded or performed below expectations. The parents, no matter who they were or what combination of sex, species or race, agreed to assume all responsibility. The Barn had done their best to ensure optimal results. The rest was up to the couple.

They signed, for if they had not the procedure would not move forward and the material collected from the couple would be incinerated or, worse, could be used at the discretion of the research team for whatever purpose they so designated.

A stimulant drink took care of any residual drowsiness from the procedure and after draining their glasses they were sent on their way. It would take six weeks before they would know if the parts taken from their bodies had produced a positive result at which point they could tell family and friends that they were decisively and deliriously expecting.

The six weeks passed in busyness, both applying themselves strenuously at work and at play. They went out each night to the brawling stations and consumed as much fire potion as was in their power to consume for they knew that, should the procedure succeed, all their merrymaking would come to an end. It was a sacrifice their friends had told them about. Things are going to change, their friends had warned, but their friends had also told them how this would not feel like a sacrifice, that they would willingly give up this and more. They would give up everything, do anything to ensure the health and welfare of the growing life for which they had assumed a hallowed obligation.

The six-week deadline came and went, producing daily tears from the Wife for every day past the due date. When she wasn't crying, she raged at the Husband for not picking up his basal coverings and putting them into the maturation receptacle, got mad at the pep up brewer when the black liquid didn't flow fast enough into her cup, and once she kicked their snuggle varmint, shocking both of them. The Husband was ready to fire up their speedtraveler and break a record zipping over to the Barn to accuse them of tampering with the Wife. He would sick the state's reinforcers on them, so help me Bezuzala, he said. This was something their friends and family did not prepare them for. This was agony.

Two more weeks passed before the fateful day when the notification came in. Yes, the procedure had been successful. In another month they were to return to the Barn to pick up their offspring.

***

It was the same red and white building, the same flowers waving gently in the wind, but for them, everything had changed. They were still nervous, but it was nervous excitement, the glow that all expectant parents exhibited. The Wife had to tell the Husband, in a voice tinged with laughter, to be careful driving the speedtraveler. She reminded him that from now on, they must ensure not only the health and well-being of their new life, they must also ensure that their own lives continued to be filled with vitality because now they were called to a higher purpose.

The waiting room was all soft edges and comfortable furniture, nothing like the sterile compartments they had experienced on their first visit. The Wife relaxed, letting the ambiance of the room fully embrace her, but the Husband found that he could not sit still. He examined a collage of pictures on the wall opposite which displayed beaming parents holding up their wondrous creations. Many different species, but each offspring beautiful, precious, and one could see from the expressions on the parents' faces, deeply loved and cherished.

A door opened up in the wall with a hushed swish and a staff member trundled in with a cart trimmed in frilly lace on which rested a shallow bowl. A soft melodious sound came from the bowl and this sound was as a siren call for the Husband and Wife. How amazing, how entrancing, how beauteous was the voice of their precious offspring. The air around them misted with a delicate scent. It was a mixture of pheromones blended from each of the three to ensure family bonding, but the Husband and Wife needed no such chemical inducement. They were already in love.

"Would you like to hold it?" asked the attendant standing next to the cart. She lifted the bowl which contained a dark earthy mixture of essential nutrients and in the center, a small waxy green nubbin. The Wife cradled the bowl, hugging it to her chest. The Husband's smile, as he cast his eyes lovingly down at the growth in the Wife's arms, was as wide as a sunbeam.

"Here is a booklet we've prepared. Inside are basic instructions. Should you need more guidance, we're just a phone call away." Success had softened the beadledom of this severe institution with its tests to pass and all its hoops to jump through. Now everyone was completely on their side.

***

It was the first day the Wife would be soloing. She had volunteered for the first half of their shared maternity leave. At the door, cradling the bowl and rocking softly, she kissed the Husband goodbye. The Husband leaned down to offer a farewell to his little sprout, a gentle touch on the topmost part. To his amazement and delight, the sprout responded with one of its sounds, a sweet musical vibration. The Wife smiled reassurance to the Husband. She had this.

Until around three o'clock in the afternoon when the musical chiming that had been charming the Wife all day turned into the clanging of a large pair of cymbals. She could hardly believe that one so little could raise such a ruckus and frantically flipped the pages in the Bank's booklet for an answer. When your growing shoot begins to clamor make sure it has plenty of water. After making sure it has plenty of water and the substratum below the bowl hasn't become wet, all should be well. If your shoot continues to clamor, try singing to it. She ran to the sink and filled up a bottle, ran back to her sprout. It drank the whole thing but, after finishing, returned to the giving off of the sharp keening noise. She stuck a finger in the substratum. It was wet. Now what? Back to the booklet.

When the substratum dampens, you need to change it with the reserve material that came with your sprout. Had the Barn given them any? She seemed to recall a bundle of things they had stuck in the trunk, the trunk they had forgotten to empty, the trunk on the speedtraveler the Husband had driven to work.

With the bowl in her arms and the sprout contained inside it still keening, she swiped the screen on the touchcom. It took forever, about seven dingbots, for the Husband to pick up. When he did she could barely hear him. He was equally deafened.

She calmly and rationally shouted her explanation over the noise their offspring made. She told him about the forgotten substratum in their speedtraveler and he promised to check. He said he'd call around and ask one of their friends in the meantime if they could swing by with some surplus from their own stash. In the meantime he tried singing over the phone.

At once, their sprout quieted. It leaned in towards the touchcom as if to be nearer to the dulcet tones of its father. The Husband's singing had the opposite effect on the Wife, who had tried singing to their sprout without success. She became squeezed between two feelings, gratitude that something had worked, and jealousy that it was the Husband who had managed it.

When her turn was over, the Wife had gotten better at caring for their shoot, but she was relieved to be returning to work with its clear and easily understood methods for determining success or failure. At the end of her first work day, having received no frantic phone calls or messages of any sort from the Husband, it was confirmed. Their offspring was a Daddy's boy. She would have to get used to it.

After two months their progeny reached a new stage of development, a milestone as the booklet called it. It had grown a tiny hand. They gave it a name, Pankaja, which means "born of mud," a transliteration of the Sanskrit, and they sent out an avalanche of images through all communication channels. Their happiness had increased ten-fold. Their child was a miracle.

In another month the swollen bud of another tiny fist began to appear exactly opposite the first. Another round of images flooded the communication pathways. Wasn't he the smartest, the cleverest, the most handsome little flower they'd ever seen? All politely agreed whether or not they thought so.

Another three weeks went by. Another swelling appeared. This was to be expected, the normal progression towards the next milestone and eventual harvesting of a fully grown, fully developed (in their case) human child. But this time they waited to send out images, for with each passing day it became clear to the couple that their offspring was developing, not a foot which would eventually grow a shin, knee and thigh, but another hand.

There was nothing in the booklet that addressed this type of unusual development, no reassuring instructions, no guidance as to how to respond. In all their late night worries, their trials and tribulations of figuring out how to care for their precious sprout in the early days of its existence, they had never called the Barn. Now they did. They called the information hotline and started babbling at once to the automated receptionist who asked them to call her Heather.

"He's got an extra hand!"

"This isn't covered in the booklet!"

"Whatever shall we do?"

All Heather wanted was to have them answer "Yes" or "No." When they had worn down their litany of catastrophe they understood, answered with the required response and reached one of the doctors.

"I agree with you. It isn't covered in the booklet. But if you refer to line 137 on page 364 of your contract in part B under, 'Ephemera,' you will see a list of temporary conditions. The extra hand should shrink and eventually fall off of its own accord."

"But why does it happen in the first place?" asked the Wife. She had the residual guilt that all mothers share and can be summed up thusly: whatever unforeseen misfortune her child experiences in life, it is always and forevermore her fault.

"Sometimes when one or the other contributor to the seedling has, shall we say, unusually robust genes, it manifests as an outgrowth such as your child is experiencing. Or, in the mixing of the genes, some protein gets turned on. It is impossible to know for certain, but I have never heard of something like this not resolving with a termination of the extra appendage. Please don't worry."

Robotic Heather broke into the line. Their time with the doctor was at an end. The couple hung up and although not entirely satisfied, tried to do what the doctor advised, which basically amounted to telling them to wait and see.

But waiting and seeing did not result in any kind of comfort. Not only had the hand not shriveled and fallen off in the time they waited, Pankaja had grown another hand, bringing the total up to four. "Four hands!" the Husband joked, "Just think how much our son will be able to get done in one day!" He had meant to lighten his Wife's load. She glared at him. In all other ways, Pankaja was developing nicely. He had the pleasing plumpness that all babies show at one time or another. He had a head, complete with eyes nose and round puckery lips. He could blow bubbles with those lips and when he did, each pair of hands met in a clumsy clapping. When he was happy, which was most of the time, he made a gurgling sound that ended in a pleasing bell-like peel. He had learned to laugh. Wasn't that also one of the milestones? But his parents did not send out messages and no one received any videos in emlets or over the touchcom.

Pankaja continued to exhibit a cheerful temperament and he continued to grow hands. He had two located on either side of his torso, two more grew out of the front and back while a third pair existed lower down where legs had been expected. A bud on the left side of his neck was hopefully regarded by his parents as an indication of illness, but ended up being another hand. By the time five nubs developed on this neck bud, growing into fat wiggly fingers, they demanded some answers.

"What are you feeding it?"

"He's not an it, he's a child and his name is Pankaja," said the Husband.

"And you followed the protocol to the letter? No substitutions, no generic brands of the substratum? Did you add something to his water bottles? Sometimes new parents learn something from other parents and then in an effort to help their sprout grow quicker, mix in an additive."

"You're making it sound like this is our fault," said the Wife.

"No, no. I'm just mentioning it because it has been known to happen. Parents get notions sometimes and they go against established, legitimate scientific precepts, so I had to ask. What else has Pankaja been doing besides growing hands?"

The Husband and Wife took turns describing their son's achievements. Pankaja was evacuating his waste in the usual fashion. They had pinned on a traditional diaper around his non-traditional limbs. He was eating with his mouth and had even started to do some "pre-talking" making many expressions of "de-de-de," "ba-ba-ba" and "mu-me-mu." He was still occasionally emitting his bell sounds, but they had become less frequent.

"Look, I know you don't want to hear this, but it sounds like little Pankaja is ready to harvest." After a few moment's pause the doctor continued, "Try and think of his unusual development as an ability, not a defect. As you may recall, differing abilities were part of our package."

The Wife became angry. She had been posting on pinbats where other parents cited their own strange tales. "There's a group forming. Have you heard about it? A group that's protesting against you people."

"Merely rants. Everyone signs the same forms. But there is one thing you can do. You can always try again. We'll even give you a discount. Bring in Pankaja and we'll incinerate."

The Wife slashed the touchcom closed. They would never do anything so vile. There was nothing more to do than to accept the situation.

And as the Husband and Wife strove to come to terms with the way their offspring had developed, Pankaja grew. His stem became a spindly stalk, barely able to support him, and certainly offered little nutrition. They had no choice but to harvest and so they did. Free from the bounds of his bowl, Pankaja began to pull himself up. Though he could not walk, if placed next to a low-lying table in a special chair, his many hands worked in an orchestrated frenzy building fantastic shapes with blocks. Even the tiniest block was not beyond his prehensile control.

"Our boy has the makings of a first-rate architect," said the Husband. The Wife looked up from her intelliscreen, smiled and returned to her work. While the Husband concentrated on childcare, taking over as soon as their nanny left for the day, she'd been absorbed in some sort of research project, tapping and swiping late into the night. It wasn't something she said much about.

Until one day as Pankaja was playing with his blocks, she came out of their bedroom and handed her intelliscreen to the Husband. There was a procedure. It was a risk. She wanted them to try it.

The article described an operation with no guarantees. The

extra appendages, after the amputation, could grow back. The desired ones many not grow in at all, despite the growth medium which needed to be applied three times a day to the four desired stump sites and the suppression gel to the other remaining stumps. Their child would have to take injections for the rest of his life and the injections could have unforeseen effects on his behavior. Physical, emotional and intellectual functioning could be forever compromised. Despite all these risks, the Wife tilted her head up to the Husband offering shining hopeful eyes. It was the same eager and loving expression she had worn on her face almost a year ago on their evening out. In the mind of the Wife, the procedure offered Pankaja a chance for a future, but the Husband wasn't so sure.

"It sounds to me like you don't want your son to get the best chance at life he can get!" she shot at him.

"I guess I'm just worried about what could happen if he goes through it. I love the little sprout, just as he is."

"And I don't?" She saw the doubt on the Husband's face and her voice softened. "Think of him as an adult when we're old and grey and he's out in the world. Yes, he has talent, but even if he became a world famous inventor, would he be happy? We accept him as he is, but would others? And after we die, what then? Will he have found a companion that also loves him just the way he is? I don't want our son to be alone."

He had not considered all these things. In the days that followed, he reviewed them. Was he being selfish, loving Pankaja the way he was now? Depriving his son of a future and the chance for a normal existence simply because he was afraid? After much discussion and many complex emotions surfacing on both sides, they came to agreement. Pankaja would undergo the procedure.

Bright lights paled their son's naked green skin. The echoes of the cymbal sound trailed on the edges of his very human cries. Pankaja lay beneath a white sheet awaiting surgery. His hands were strapped to a board. Big round tears sprang from his eyes. His parent's each held out fingers near the straps and their son gripped them as the doctor began administering anesthesia. Their child would be firmly asleep throughout the whole thing. He would not suffer. And in a little while, the injections and the stump balms would do their jobs.

After five hours, they were allowed to see their son in the recovery room. Pankaja had been reduced to a head and torso, the lower half of which was encased in a plastic bag filled with the familiar dark substrate. A mask covered his nose and mouth with a long tube attached to a machine making a sucking sound. His swollen eyes peeked through blue eyelids, half closed. Dark circles bloomed underneath. Both the Wife and the Husband held out a finger and then realized their infant son did not have the means to grasp. Pankaja's eyelids closed shut. The sucking sound continued. The plastic chairs upon which the Wife and the Husband sat continued to be hard and uncomfortable.

"Here is a packet for you containing the materials you'll need and instructions for home care. As soon as he's stable, he'll be discharged. Don't worry! You've got this. It's just like starting over, only this time, after a little while, he'll look just like you."

Since they hadn't told anyone about Pankaja's unusual development, none of their friends or relatives knew about his surgery. This was how the Wife had wanted it and the Husband went along. It made it hard to do everything that was needed since asking for help would mean divulging the secret and they could not afford respite care. They became short with one another, double checking, "Did you remember the 5 a.m. injection?" "Have you made sure to apply the salve to all seven stumps?" And one time the Wife caught the Husband mumbling to himself, "All this and for what?"

But Pankaja did improve. He returned to the cheerful little toddler he had been before, and after a little while new buds formed, a pair on the left at the place for hands and arms. A pair lower down at the place for feet and limbs. And nothing more. The Husband and Wife were overjoyed. The surgery, all they had forced their son to go through worked! The Wife lost interest in the pinbats she had been following and came to the conclusion that all they really were was rants. The Husband began to dream about games of catch in which Pankaja ran and leapt. They measured the growth of these four buds each day, hopeful for the day they could at last resume the steady stream of pictures.

About the time they began to see the stubs of fingers and toes, the stalks that should have continued to develop with elbows and knees coming next began to thin. The Husband and Wife stepped up their efforts and the Wife returned to her research. Was there something more they could do? The words of the doctor's warnings, not to follow other parents ideas returned, but she ignored them and when she could not find anything new, any new directions, something experimental to try, she grew frantic. It didn't help matters that Pankaja's condition continued to deteriorate. His torso thinned, his eyes began to sink into their eye sockets. And most of all, there was no longer the sound of babbling and no peels of laughter came from his lips. No sound at all, except for an occasional gasp when they changed his dressings. Pankaja had gone from a glowing thriving creature to one that was failing to thrive.

This time, it was the Husband who called the doctors. The Wife was too overcome with guilt and grief. And just as at the

Barn, forms were cited, the ones they had signed agreeing not to prosecute, acknowledging that there were no guarantees. The Husband said he understood. He reassured the doctor they hadn't done anything beyond what the hospital had recommended for follow up care. In a voice dry with desperation he asked if there was anything further they could do. No, they were very sorry, but no there wasn't.

So Pankaja withered as the Wife and the Husband watched, still applying salve, still changing the dressings until it was obvious that their actions had no effect. And at the funeral, friends and family gazed on the serene face of the little boy now at peace, the only part of his body visible in the coffin where he lay. They offered sympathy, telling them they could try again, not the right thing to say, but no one knows what to say at a time like this. "You did everything you could," someone else said to the Wife who burst into tears.

"Pankaja? I've never heard of the name before. How did you come up with it?" said a colleague standing next to the Husband who gripped the coffin's railing.

"It was my grandfather's name," the Husband said. "I wanted him to have something from my family."

"He has your forehead. And your eyes." The colleague scrutinized the Husband. "As a matter of fact, he looks just like you." Then Husband's own eyes filled with tears. His hands trembled as he released them from their grip. Turning away from the colleague, he let the tears roll down his cheeks.

Goners

Hannah Sternberg

Hannah Sternberg is the author of two novels, Bulfinch and Queens of All the Earth. She also plays bass and cello in Daamsel, a femme-fronted indie rock band.

My cousin Jimmy said he had an easy job and an easier life out on the North Carolina shore. Prospects were lean in Wisconsin, so I was open to suggestions. His was simple: I'd blow in whenever I could make it, and he'd set me up. We shared everything in childhood (even a name) and answering his call felt like a return to a time when things were better.

I hitchhiked my way out from Milwaukee. Jimmy had told me that whenever I arrived, I'd find the key under the doormat. I was to await his return from work, at which point we would knock beers, find ourselves winsome lasses, and repeat every night until we decided to move on. This plan did not require the exchange of travel details or the establishment of a specific arrival date, so I took my time weaving about the small towns of the Great Plains, seeing a bit of what there was to see along the way.

Things went smoothly until the last leg of the journey. I found a trucker who gave me a ride from Raleigh nearly all the way to the shore, but he said there was no Aubrey, North Carolina.

I said, "Maybe you haven't heard of it. It's a small place, just off 64 before you cross the bridge to Nag's Head?"

The trucker shook his head.

"Ain't no such place," he said.

"My cousin gave me directions."

"Good for him. I can get you as far as the exit."

"Fair enough. Much traffic that way?"

The driver shrugged.

"Depends," he replied.

I ran over Jimmy's directions in my head, feeling for the first time a prickle of anxiety about not sharing my travel plans. Too late now. My phone had bricked in Missouri, after an incident involving a toilet at a bar, and as I drew closer to my destination, the sense of freedom I'd gained had started to wear thin. I wanted a real sleep in a real house after a real meal.

What I got was a sandy backwoods road off the exit the trucker had agreed to drop me at. "Depends" had been his gentle way of letting me know ain't nobody out here. When I climbed down, he said, "Good luck finding Osprey," and I knew he still didn't believe it existed.

Jimmy must have anticipated this, because his directions included a footpath shortcut through a small national forest that hugged Croatan Sound. Jimmy said this was easier than traveling along the roads, especially if there weren't any rides to hail along the way. The town of Aubrey was a small, inhabited pocket of land just on the other side of the forest. I fingered my pocketknife as I trekked along the grass-choked lane. It was late afternoon and my shirt stuck to my back. I had the lousy, gummy feeling of having sat in cars for too long, and I'd forgotten to grab my water bottle when I hopped out of the trucker's cab. The desolation and the trucker's doubt got inside my head. When you're walking along an empty trail you've never walked before, time loses its shape and fear rushes into all the extra minutes you manufacture.

With no watch, and my phone dead, I don't know how long it took me to get there, but as afternoon tilted into dusk, the trail finally widened and I saw buildings through the trees. A one-pump gas station marked the edge of town, just as Jimmy said it would. I didn't see anyone outside, but I thought it might be Sunday. Days had blurred together on the road, and with no job, I'd stopped caring.

I followed Jimmy's directions faithfully, and faithfully they led me straight to his door. So far I had not encountered a single soul in the town of Aubrey, North Carolina, as night settled quickly. If it weren't for the faint sounds of activity inside some of the houses I passed, I would have agreed with the trucker: this place hardly existed at all.

Jimmy's home was on the beach, perched between a strand of pine trees and the dunes. It stood on stilts, like a lot of houses in hurricane country. The ground floor was the garage, walled in with trellis to allow sand and water to flow through. A porch had been built out on the side, for grilling. An exterior set of wooden stairs led to the front door on the second floor, where the living spaces were. The floodlight at the top of the stairs was burned out, and I didn't see any other lights on inside the house. In the moonlight I saw the stairs well enough to get my bearings, and climbed up. I found the key under the mat, just like Jimmy told me.

I fumbled my way through his door, and switched on the first light I found.

It was a shabby little hole. Beaded curtain to the kitchen. Nubbly couches smelling not-faintly of cat piss and weed. Broken TV in the corner with a massive crack across its screen, now serving as a plant stand to several perishing cacti.

I suspected Jimmy had hit the one bar in town, and would get home when he got home. I let myself into the spare bedroom—its door hung open and I saw it was far too uncluttered to be inhabited by Jimmy. I threw the window open, letting in the cleansing ocean air. I could live with Jimmy as long as I had this space, this sparse, pure room.

The window of my room overlooked the roof of the back porch. I crawled through the window onto the roof. I sat up lazily, back propped against the house, one knee bent. Through a break in the brambles that were struggling to be trees, I could see the dunes that separated us from the sea, bristling with razor grass and cattails. Though I couldn't see the ocean, I could hear it. I leaned my head back and closed my eyes.

My neatness was the only way in which I differed from Jimmy. Our mothers, who were sisters, looked exactly alike, and so did we—so alike that people often mistook us not only for brothers, but for twins. My mother married a man named Monroe and Jimmy's mother married a man named Madison and they both thought it would be noble to name their sons James, so in that we were similar as well. I went by my full name.

We grew up like brothers, too. I think sometimes we read each other's thoughts. It was how we managed to cause such utter mayhem in our schools and neighborhood. If we were in completely different places I could sense if he was in trouble and I'd go cover for him.

When we were eighteen we got tattoos together, our initials on the insides of our wrists. "A proud tattoo," he'd called it. "No hiding it." It also hurt like hell.

At the time, the pain bound us together, but later it seemed like that was the last time we'd be so close. After we got the tattoos, Jimmy started drifting. I couldn't tell what had changed. He went from being my brother to being my cousin, just another relative. Then he moved out here, where none of our blood lived, and I didn't hear much from him until this year when he invited me to live with him.

The sense of his absence, after wandering the deserted town, sent an uncanny finger up my spine. My eyes snapped open and I decided to check out the beach and shake off some of my dark thoughts.

It wasn't hard to climb over the dunes, answering the bay's soft call of whish, whish, boom. Any trace of worry was erased by the sand's sweet erosion. It wasn't that I stopped wondering where Jimmy might be; I felt he was right here, that he was me. It was like walking into a party and asking, "Has anybody seen me lately?" It made me want to laugh.

I saw a heap of rags on the beach ahead and wandered over to investigate. I walked faster when I saw the heap begin to move. By the time I reached it, a person had begun to emerge. Her hair, long and wet, was ashy blonde, and in the moonlight she could have blended right into the sand. Ocean-blue eyes opened wide and wondering. Her threadbare clothes hung from soft shoulders. I broke into a run, kicking up sand. When she saw me, turned and held her arms open. I thought it as a plea for help, but when I arrived at her side, she embraced me as if we were old friends.

"Um, hi," I murmured, finding my cheek resting on her hair as she buried her face in my shoulder. Her shoulders shook and I couldn't tell if it was laughter or sobs, but when her face lifted from my chest I saw it was a little of both.

"I'm out," she said, her voice carrying a faint, undefinable accent. "Thank you, thank you."

"I'm just here," I said. "Are you from Aubrey? Do you need help?"

This made her laugh harder.

"It doesn't matter," she said. "I'm no one. And you are too."

"You need help," I said. "You got a home?"

The laughter became tears again, as quickly as clouds shifting across the sun.

"Don't make me go back," she said. "She can't stop me now."

"Okay, okay," I soothed. "No one's making you go anywhere, except someplace warm and safe. Can you walk? Are you hurt?"

"I was in the surf when I woke up," she said. "Stung by some jellyfish, I think." She began to lift one edge of the garment she was wearing, revealing a creamy pale leg lashed with red welts.

"Lemme take you to my place," I said. "Then we'll figure out what to do."

I never noticed until later how smoothly, how easily, it became "my place."

***

For a lot of my life I've been a little bit tweaked. Anxious fellow, they said. Acts out. I don't know what it is, but when I get that screeching feeling inside, I go to a house in my head. It's a cottage on the shore where I am utterly alone. People exist outside an invisible barrier and I can hear them play, but they don't come close.

As I walked up to Jimmy's house again, seeing it from the top of the dunes, it sank in: this is the house I had always imagined. The similarity would have made me shudder, but I was too occupied with the woman hanging off my arm as if she'd never learned to walk on her own.

Inside the house, there was still no sign of Jimmy.

"Sit down anywhere," I told the woman.

I left her and went to scope out the kitchen for coffee, squaring my shoulders as I did so, hoping she could see my broad back. The coffeemaker was broken, so I put on a pot of water to heat on the stove. When I turned around, she was sitting on the living room floor, cross-legged. In the light, I saw she wore a ragged kimono-style robe, and no shoes.

"Yeah, I wouldn't touch the furniture either," I said. "It's my cousin Jimmy's place. I take it as I find it."

She didn't reply, but seemed lost in the cracks between the floor boards. Something about her tugged at me, made me forget about the coffee. Made me want to stay inside the sphere of her presence, a golden orb that embraced anyone within an arm's distance of her. I stepped toward her, and sank to the floor by her side.

"What's your story?" I said. "What were you doing on the beach?"

"What?" she asked, startled from her trance.

"How did you wind up on the beach?" I asked again. "What were you getting away from? Do you need me to call someone? Are you hurt?" She giggled uncontrollably. The laughter built up and up and over until she covered her face with her hands and leaned forward, her hair falling around her like a curtain, close enough that I could smell the salt in it. I started laughing too. I don't know why. Probably because she was so damn pretty.

"I should be at home!" she said, gasping.

"Do you need help getting back home?" I asked. "Not that I'm chasing you out. You look great on my floor."

The smile dropped from her face like a rock, and her laughing stopped so abruptly my ears rang.

"No," she said. "I don't want to go back there."

"Okay," I said, trying to be soothing. "No one's making you go anywhere you don't want to go."

She stood up, hair flying, and took a step back from me like a frightened animal.

"Do you promise?" she asked.

"Cross my heart," I replied, rising slowly with my hands up.

A smile flowed over her face like the rivers of her hair.

"I get to live on the outside now," she said, spinning around once to take in the room. If this was an upgrade, I wondered what the place she came from looked like.

"Was someone harming you?" I asked. She nodded. "Do you want me to call the police?" I continued.

"We don't have police," she said. "Just a night watchman."

I took a deep breath.

"Do you have any family? Friends you could talk to?" I asked.

She shook her head. "I've been alone for a long time. I used to have friends, when I took turns with Cassie. But after mother died, I haven't seen anybody but her."

"Who's Cassie?"

"My sister."

"Is she the one who was harming you?"

"Not on purpose, usually. She just forgot my turn."

"I don't understand what you're talking about. I think you might have a concussion. Have you taken anything? Any drugs?" She didn't smell like alcohol.

"I just haven't talked to someone in a long time," she said. "I think I forgot how."

"Follow my finger with your eyes," I said, waving it slowly in front of her face. She tracked it easily. "What's your name?"

"Tess."

"Do you have a last name?"

"I don't think so. I've always been Tess from the lighthouse."

I dropped my hand.

"You don't know your last name?"

"We don't really need them out here. There aren't that many people, and after a while you forget."

I lifted her wrist and felt her pulse. As far as my limited knowledge went, it seemed strong and healthy.

I heard a hiss in the kitchen and realized the pot was boiling over.

"Are you injured?" I asked. "Besides those jellyfish stings?"

She shook her head again.

"Okay. You're going to spend the night here, sleep off...whatever you've had, and we'll work this out in the morning. Hop in the shower to wash the stingers off and I'll get you some vinegar."

I fixed up some tea while I listened to the shower running in the bathroom. I hoped Jimmy didn't have anything worth stealing around here. I found a bottle of apple cider vinegar in the kitchen cabinet, and left it on the floor outside the bathroom door.

When Tess emerged, I'd made up the couch with some spare blankets I found in a closet, after shaking the sand out of them on the landing outside. I placed her mug of tea on the floor beside the couch.

"I'll see you in the morning," I said.

"It's just like I imagined it would be," she said, a radiant smile spread across her face.

I raised my eyebrows and turned to my own room. It wasn't until I lay down that I realized, after all my offers to call someone, that I didn't even think Jimmy had a landline set up. I left the door ajar so I could hear it if Jimmy came in or Tess snuck out. I wondered what Jimmy would think when he came home and saw her.

He probably wouldn't think anything at all.

***

By the time the morning light touched Tess on the couch, she seemed to belong there. I got up early, and surveyed the kitchen for breakfast things. All I found was some expired instant oatmeal.

Tess appeared to be sleeping deeply. If she woke up, and decided to leave while I was gone, I wouldn't be any worse off than when I'd got here. But I found myself hoping she'd stay.

I walked to the corner convenience store I'd seen the night before. In the daylight I got a better look around. Aubrey was a bleached-out beach town like an old postcard that had been left out in the sun too long. Everything had a thin patina of salt on it, and I was pretty sure if I looked behind any shutter I'd find paint ten shades darker than the rest of the house. It was normally the kind of place I liked – dusty, unobtrusive, unapologetically strange – but its quietness was too perfect.

There were no cars anywhere.

The store was deserted except for the ancient guardian of the cash register, who may have been a mannequin for all he did to acknowledge my existence. I grabbed some essentials, hugging them in my arms because I forgot to get a basket. I dumped it all on the counter, and the old man made his first move, to ring me up.

"You can't just quit your job like that, Jimmy," he said toothlessly.

"I think you're confusing me with my cousin," I said. "We look alike."

"It's a work day. You should be at the hardware store. They're talking about you, Jimmy," the old man said.

"You got the wrong guy," I muttered between my teeth, but I couldn't go anywhere until he took the money from my hands.

"That's impossible," the geezer said.

"Then surely this will be remembered as the day that pigs fly," I said. "Gimme my change."

The old man pulled the lever on the register and methodically counted out bills. He handed me my bag and my change with a scowl and I got the hell out.

When I got back, Tess was up and pacing the apartment. She threw herself at me when I walked in, grasping me by the shoulders.

"Did anybody see you?" she asked. "Were you seen?"

I held up the bag.

"I got breakfast," I said. "My cousin doesn't keep a lot around, apparently."

"No," she said, looking stricken. "You shouldn't have gone out without waking me."

I stepped back, shaking out of her grip.

"I don't have to ask you permission to leave my own house," I snapped.

"It's too late," she said, falling backward onto the couch. "How many people saw you?"

"Just the old guy in the store," I said. "He thought I was my cousin."

"No," she said, softly this time. "It's already happened."

I didn't know what I feared, but I tasted something sour at the back of my throat.

"Do you know my cousin?" I said. "What's so wrong with someone thinking I'm him?" I put the bags down, the sour taste now overpowering my mouth. "Did he do something? Did something happen to him?"

Tess choked back a sob.

"Maybe if you don't know, there's still a chance," she said. "Do you have a car?"

"I hitchhiked in," I said.

"How far in?" she asked.

"I got dropped off at the exit off 64."

"Did you come alone?"

"Yes," I said.

"That's too bad for you," she whispered. "But we might catch them."

"Where the hell is Jimmy?" I said. "You clearly know something."

Tess got up.

"I have to show you," she said.

"Is he dead?" I stood between her and the door.

She laughed bitterly.

"No," she said. "If he's still here, you could say he's remarkably well-preserved."

Tess stopped herself with a hand to her mouth.

"I'm sounding just like my sister now," she said. "It's happening."

"Just show me what you're going to show me," I said, stepping aside and letting her out the door.

Tess walked out with such confidence that we were halfway down the road before I remembered she wasn't wearing shoes.

She took me back to the path I'd used to get in, with an ease and precision that made me think she'd walked this way many times before.

I hesitated on the edge of the trail. I didn't think she could overpower me, but what if she had someone waiting to rob me? That seemed unlikely, and anyway I had nothing worth stealing. It was worth it to follow her, if I learned something about where Jimmy had gone.

Any trail seems much shorter the second time you walk it, especially if you're no longer alone. In five minutes we were under pine trees, and in another twenty minutes I thought I recognized some of the turnings that came close to the highway exit. Tess stayed slightly ahead of me, impervious to the sharp rocks and needles under her feet, striding purposefully. I started to lose my sense of direction when I realized I should have been hearing highway traffic by now. I had definitely seen a distinctive rock that I'd passed yesterday, close to the exit; a smooth outcropping with one jagged portion standing in the middle, like a sundial. We hadn't taken any forks in the path, nor had we turned around, but I started to notice other little landmarks I'd seen before—a pile of stones carefully stacked by a hiker, a single mountain laurel at the edge of the path—that led me to believe we were now walking back towards town.

I was correct. In another fifteen minutes we reached the edge of the woods and I saw the path cut through the tall grass to the abandoned one-pump gas station.

"We missed the turn off to the highway," I said. "It must have been a side track I didn't notice somewhere."

Tess just looked at me, sadly. I headed back into the woods, and this time she walked by my side, swinging her hand so it sometimes brushed mine.

We made it back to the sundial and I started hunting for a small footpath leading off the main trail. The smooth bed of pine needles offered no clues. I thought I spotted a way between the trees that seemed slightly indented, and took that. Tess trailed with a sigh. I felt confident I'd found it.

To my surprise, in a few moments the footpath dumped me out into the tall grass again, just across from the one-pump gas station.

I started to hear a rushing sound in my ears.

"Where's Jimmy?" I asked.

Tess began to cry.

"He's gone," she said. "They're both gone."

"Who did he leave with? What do you know?"

"With my sister," she choked out. "He went with my sister. She kept me in the lighthouse, locked in a room, but I could hear things through the door. I heard your—his voice, when he visited her, and I knew what they were planning. But I hoped we could get out first." Tess's voice cracked so badly she barely got the last words out.

"Well, why can't we just follow them? Where did they go?" I took a deep breath and tried to muffle the screeching sound in my head, but the heat and lack of food and the trails that led nowhere made it difficult.

She looked at me with a tear-streaked face.

"You can walk that trail as many times as you like, try as many paths as you dare, and they'll all lead back here, like a closed loop."

I left her there in the grass and set off on the trail at a run this time. Halfway to the sundial I tripped on a root and twisted my ankle, but I got up with a curse and kept limping on as fast as I could. The sun was high enough now that it was hard to use it as a reference point, but as much as possible I tried to keep my narrow shadow in front of me, heading west toward the highway. I lost it somewhere in the shade of the pines, and emerged five yards away from where Tess was crouched at the edge of the meadow.

I turned around, the pain in my ankle nauseating, and found the trail one more time. Not far from the edge of the trees, I put my bad foot into a hidden depression in the ground and wrenched it again. My vision went black and I fell heavily to my knees, heaving.

I felt Tess's gentle arms around me, lifting my arm over her shoulder. Eventually, we rose together and she supported me back to the crooked house on the beach.

I sat on the couch in a daze, gradually aware of the sounds of Tess moving items in the kitchen. She reappeared with toast and sausages and a huge glass of water and a small bottle of whiskey.

"Explain," I said, taking a sip of the water.

"You know how water eddies in a corner of a cave or rock formation that traps the current?" she said. I nodded. I'd almost drowned in one of those as a kid, rafting on a family vacation in Colorado. "Time eddies here," Tess continued. "It got stuck. And now we're stuck in it."

I picked up the glass of water again, found I couldn't breathe, set it down, and took the whiskey instead.

"What happens?" I asked.

"Nothing ever changes and no one leaves. We've been living the same lives over and over again, new generations but the same roles. Every cycle, there's a woman keeping the lighthouse. She falls for a drifter in the beach house, and she gets pregnant. He drowns, she raises their daughter alone in the lighthouse. She is the new lighthouse keeper. The hardware store manager falls asleep with the generator on and asphyxiates. We've been through three of those in my lifetime; this batch don't seem to last long. The couple on the corner of Roanoke Lane and Juniper Street start building a boat every spring. They work on it every weekend, but it never gets done, and then one year it gets washed away in a hurricane and they start over again. The Williams sisters down the street start learning the piano...they've been playing for years and never progressed, but then again, sometimes people aren't very good, right? Only, every generation a new pair of sisters takes the house, and they start learning the piano..."

I started to tune out Tess's voice. Slowly, I got up, grabbing a street hockey stick from the corner as a crutch. I hobbled down the stairs. Swallowing my pain (and a little more whiskey from the bottle, which I'd taken with me), I made my way into the hardware store I'd seen a few storefronts down from the convenience mart, the one where Jimmy was supposed to work.

It was cool inside the hardware store, and a furry coat of dust covered the items on the top shelves. I tried to focus on the familiarity of the bins of screws and nails, to bring myself down so I could ask someone sane about all this.

"Is this some kind of joke?" a roughneck in coveralls hollered at me, voicing my thoughts exactly. He circled the front desk and got up in my face. His nametag said Mark. "You're late, you're drunk, and you're maimed?"

"Yessir," I slurred.

"We're supposed to get a shipment today," Mark shouted. "What the hell am I supposed to do with you?"

I shrugged.

"What's my name?" I asked.

"Dear lord, Jimmy, you're far gone for this time of the morning," Mark said.

I smiled.

"I don't think that shipment's going to come in," I said.

"What is going on with you?"

"I think you should fire Jimmy," I said. "He's a pretty bad employee."

"Go home and sleep it off," Mark said. "I'll see you tomorrow."

I turned haplessly to find Tess behind me; she'd followed me.

"Hey Cassie," Mark said.

Tess flinched. She took my hand and led me out of the hardware store without acknowledging Mark's greeting.

"Something went wrong with my cycle," Tess said, following me. "My mother had twins. She wasn't supposed to have twins. The lighthouse keeper had never had twins."

"It broke the pattern," I said.

"The pattern nearly broke us," Tess said. "Anytime we went somewhere together, Cassie and I, some kind of accident happened, something that could have killed one of us. Eventually, my mother started taking us out separately, only one at a time. We took turns. When mother died, Cassie decided she didn't want to take turns anymore."

She was staring at the lighthouse on the rock.

"She trapped you there?" I asked.

Tess nodded.

"I slipped out once or twice, but the second time I did it, I almost got struck by lightning on the beach."

"How did you get out this time?" I asked, afraid I was already halfway to guessing the answer.

"They let me out," she said. "I think they let me out to trap you."

I wanted to say his name but it wouldn't come out. Tess continued for me, keeping pace as I limped down the street, passing folk on their porches, looking at them engaged in their daily activities—sanding a railing, washing a car, weeding a garden. Slowly, they lifted their heads to look back at him.

"Cassie didn't think about escaping until Jimmy got here. It hadn't been done before, no one knew if it was possible. But when Jimmy learned he was the new drifter, and he learned what happened to the drifter every time, he had an idea. Maybe this place will let you go if you have a replacement. That meant Cassie could have been free all along, but by the time she learned that, they were deep into each other. She wanted to leave with him, so he invited you here. I don't know how they watched for you, but one night Cassie gave me something that made me fall asleep, and I woke up on the sand, like you found me. I think they figured once you saw me, you'd stay at least a night to make sure I was alright. And that would give them enough time to get out."

"You knew? You knew that was the plan and you still let me stay?" I asked, blood boiling.

"I didn't know I was the decoy. I just knew they were going to run away as soon as you hit town. I figured the rest out today."

I wanted to be angry at Tess because it was better than being angry at Jimmy. I could stand to have my heart broken by her.

We were at the end of the road. A meager curb bordering a gravel lot held back the sand of the dunes. The last house on the lane stood empty, one loose window shutter clapping in the wind. There was a woodpile under a little shelter next to the trellised garage. I picked up the ax that hung from the wall next to it.

Tess's eyes went wide.

"If you do it, it'll just start again with someone new," she said.

I brought the ax down on the trellis of the garage. I hacked until I made a hole big enough to climb through. It was hard, without the leverage of two steady feet, but I kept reminding myself I had all the time in the world. Neighbors put down their paintbrushes and their sponges and their trowels to stare at me, but no one moved.

Inside, I found what I was looking for. A two-seater kayak.

"Help me with this," I said, hopping painfully as I tossed the oars through the hole in the wall.

Tess climbed in wordlessly and helped me drag the kayak through the hole. Splinters tore the backs of my hands, but I didn't care anymore. Tess's face was resigned and sad. She knew what I was trying to do, and I think she knew what was going to happen, too.

We dragged the kayak up the dunes. The neighbors' stares swiveled to follow us, the only motion they made. I dropped to my knees, crawling to drag the boat because my ankle wouldn't take the weight. Thorny dune brambles tore at my legs.

I stayed on my knees until we'd dragged the kayak out to the edge of the bay, floating far enough into the water that it wouldn't get stuck aground once our weight was in it. I flipped it the first time I tried to get on, filling my mouth and nose with salt water, kicking to stay afloat with my bad leg until stars burst in my eyes. The second time, I made it, and I felt Tess slide into the seat behind me.

I took a single stroke and felt searing pain up my leg. I forgot that when you kayak, you leverage your arm strength against the stability of your feet and bottom in the boat. I extended my bad leg, relaxing it, and put all my weight into my good leg as I took another pull on the oars. This time we surged forward.

Tess was rowing behind me. We made for the lighthouse. I thought, if we could pull past it, that would be the proof I needed that we'd broken free. I strained and strained, but the current was always stronger than us. I turned the boat outward, toward the center of the bay, hoping to cut across the current and find calmer waters. But when I took a moment to rest my arms, eyes fixed on the thin gray line of the opposite shore, we drifted. By the time I looked over my shoulder, in what felt like moments, we were in the lee of the lighthouse again.

I rested my oar across the boat and let the waves take us in to shore, resting my tattooed wrist upward to the sky in surrender.

Tess rested behind me. The current bobbed us up to the promontory the lighthouse was built upon.

I closed my eyes, feeling the proximity of land over my left shoulder. And I heard it; a boom of the rising tide breaking against hidden hollow places, and another kind of sound, one that raised the hairs on the back of my neck.

I knew that down there was the tide that nearly killed me as a child; the tide that destroyed every drifter who came to this town. It was the sound Jimmy used to say he heard when he knew I was about to get in trouble. It was the roaring sound I'd heard in my ears my whole life when everything seemed too clear and baffling all at once. All those times, when I'd imagined the house on the beach as a way to find peace.

It was calling me to go down, down, down to the place I had always associated with peace.

I laid my head back on Tess's lap, feeling the boat bob under us, gently knocking against the rocks.

"How long do we have together?" I asked.

Baug's Hollow

Cathrin Hagey

Cathrin Hagey is a writer and editor based in western Canada.

Henrike wore her sealskin robe, secured at the throat by a tri-pod pin of bronze, a coming-of-age gift from her grandmother many years earlier. Henrike wanted to be certain that she would reunite with Baug, in death, and that, together, they would greet their ancestors under the watchful eyes of Odin and Frigg.

But Hen, as she had been fondly called, was less certain about anything than she had ever been in her life. She could no longer make out the boundary between sea and sky, could no more read her husband's face than she had the parchment upon which they scratched their signs to seal their marriage so long ago, could barely recall the plump flesh of her only child upon which she had planted kiss after kiss after kiss.

There was no certainty for Hen as she bent her head against the hot barbs of frozen rain and gained her way, step by step, toward Baug's hollow, the burial pit he had prepared for the two of them in the side of troll hill. There was only hope. Hope that death would come like sleep. Hope that Baug's spirit, hovering alone somewhere above the sea, would find land and seek her out.

When Hen reached the hollow, she stumbled and fell into it, crushing her ribs against the ridges of ice that had formed, without knowing she had broken her ankle, for the pain of it was shouted out by the pain in other parts.

Hen was barely conscious at the bottom of the pit, but she was somewhat aware of the pin at her throat and the stabbing, icy rain against her forehead. And then she was aware of nothing at all.

***

"You should have told me we have company, before I drank all the fish wine."

The troll queen, as tall as a standing sheep and as wide as two, shook her rooty finger at her smaller, yellower nephew, and then banged her head against the table for emphasis.

"We don't," said the nephew, Grigg, with more gusto than sense. "Not really."

The troll queen raised her head and cradled it in her large, square hands. "What is that supposed to mean?"

"It means there's someone here, someone who doesn't live here, but she's kind of, sort of... dead."

"Well, dead company's better than no company at all." The troll queen pushed her chair back as she stood, groaning from the effort of straightening her back. Grigg ran to pull her chair clear away. "I want to see this company with my own eyes."

The queen and her nephew, being small cave-trolls, rolled and tumbled their way along the cave's tentacle passageways. He led the way; she grunted and groaned after him. Before too long, they stopped. Grigg dropped to all fours and crawled through a hole that was small, even by small cave-troll reckoning. The queen did the same, threatening, "There'd better be treasure, or something better, at the end of this."

They found themselves standing, not tall, but standing in a chamber that the troll queen had never seen before.

"How did you find this?" she asked.

Grigg said nothing. With his mossy thighs exposed as he raised his winter tunic to avoid splashing it in the icy water at the center of the chamber, he led her to a hollowed-out place adjacent to a glittering cave wall.

"What the...?" cried the queen. For lying in the hollow place, looking every bit as regal as the troll goddess herself, was a woman, a human woman, the likes of which had never been seen inside troll hill.

"You see?" said Grigg.

"Of course I see. I'm not blind like your mother." The troll queen instantly regretted her tone, for her sister's inner sight was legendary.

"Who is she?"

The troll queen thought for a moment, scratching the scaly palms of her hands in a gesture that revealed, to her nephew's nervous eye, that she was wary.

"Fetch your mother," said the troll queen at last, not eager to admit that her sister's powers were greater than her own in a case like this. She turned and watched Grigg crawl back through the hole and disappear from sight.

The sound of Grigg's voice, singing a merry troll tune, echoed back to the troll queen's ears and only magnified her sense of defeat. It was, in truth, her sister who led the remnant of what had once been a great troll kingdom, though the crown belonged to her by order of birth.

The troll queen was studying the face of the strange, still woman, when Grigg returned, guiding his sightless mother through the hole that led to the chamber.

"Greetings, Aghi," said the troll queen.

"Greetings to you, dear ruler," replied a small being whose wisps of silvery hair bounced gaily, like tiny dancers around her head.

The queen couldn't help but silently note that her nephew was always at ease when his mother was about. Indeed, their entire band of cave trolls were, it seemed to the queen, when she was being honest with herself.

"Can you tell us who this woman is, where she came from, what she's doing here?" asked the queen.

Grigg led his mother closer to the still form of the human woman. Aghi stretched out her arms and spread her fingers, which she then placed on the woman's chest. She opened her blind eyes, wide.

"What do you see?" asked the troll queen.

"She's alive, though she's very old, for a human. And she's wounded." Aghi began to walk around the woman while holding the palms of her hands a finger's width above the woman's body. "I can bring her back. Her ancestors haven't a firm grip on her yet."

Aghi sniffed the woman's plaited hair and then placed her own soft, lumpy cheek against the woman's furrowed one.

"Who?" The troll queen's eyes bulged. Her impatience was deeply etched into her heart-shaped face. "Who is she?"

***

Hen sat on a low stool made entirely of carved stone and ate whatever the creatures before her offered. She knew they were trolls, for they had told her so as soon as she had awakened. Her first inclination had been to believe that she had died and gone to the afterlife, but the flow of blood in her limbs, better than she had felt in years, and her renewed joy in the simple pleasure of tasting fruit and flesh, were sure signs that she was bound to earth.

"Tell us about yourself, my dear," said the troll queen. "We haven't had one of your kind here in... well, I don't think we've ever had your kind here. We're not too fond of humans."

Hen thought that the three trolls around the table were staring at her as though she were the most offensive thing they had ever seen.

Aghi added, "I would like to know how you passed through the cave wall. I have a suspicion, but you should tell us about yourself first."

"Me, too," added the troll queen. "I don't want this to ever happen again." Aghi elbowed her in the navel, and the troll queen growled under her breath.

"I don't understand," said Hen. "No one can pass through a wall."

"My son and I have been studying that wall—"

"The first I've heard about it," interrupted the queen, grunting with displeasure.

"It's full of magic," blurted Grigg, and then his mother hushed him.

"I know nothing of magic," said Hen. "I'm a fisher's wife. My husband was lost at sea in a winter storm. My daughter lives far away with her new family." She looked around the table and saw that the trolls were attentive. "I felt very old and afraid. I didn't want to face another winter alone. I believed it was time to go and meet my grandmothers."

"But you came here," said the troll queen. "You couldn't have accidently stumbled into our cave. Our grandmothers took measures to make sure of that." Then she made a show of brushing her hands together as if to sweep away all thoughts of human invasion.

"I knew about troll hill, but I didn't believe the stories. I never saw a troll with my own eyes."

Then Hen explained how Baug had refused to leave their cottage to join their daughter and her husband as they could have, further up the fjord. And Baug had prepared the hollow to take them to the afterlife when their time came. When Baug failed to return from the sea, Hen had entered the hollow alone, knowing that she would die from the cold and then meet him again somewhere between earth and stars.

When Hen was done, the three trolls stared at her as if a tree had sprouted from her head.

"Baug?" said the troll queen.

"Baug," Aghi echoed.

"My dear Baug," whispered Hen, her eyes filling with tears.

"Uncle Baug?" Grigg sprang from his seat, pattered to Hen's side, and stood before her. "I've never met him, but I've heard the stories. He left us, you know. Married a human... oh." The dawning significance of the woman's presence showed in his eyes.

Hen gaped at him.

The troll queen moved forward to take her nephew's place, nudging him with her knobby elbow. "Have you come to steal my crown?"

"I don't understand," said Hen. "How do you know Baug?"

"He was my brother," replied the troll queen, gruffly. "And my uncle," added Grigg. Aghi nodded, silently.

***

Hen was treated to a round of fish wine, a spare cask of which had been found, and was soon soothed by its gentle burn on the way down, if not by its acrid aroma. Aghi added to her calm by patting her hand as the troll queen told their version of Baug, who was more mysterious at this moment to Hen than he had ever seemed since she had first set eyes on him, when she was a girl of fifteen.

"He was odd from the start," said the troll queen. "And I remember, though he was older than me. He was overly large, had a straight nose, quite ugly really. And he liked to wander far outside the cave, as if it were the old days when trolls could get away with such freedom in human realms. Our Pa put a stop to that, or so we thought."

Aghi continued to pat Hen's hand. "Baug was a great troll and a good brother."

The queen huffed. "But I'm sure you remember that Pa told

Baug to make a choice between cave and sky, between family and the world of men."

"He should have become king of the trolls," said Grigg, "but he didn't."

While the troll queen told the story of Baug, Hen felt that she had found a way to hold onto her husband for a little while longer. She began to understand that she had not known him as completely as she had believed. There was more to discover. She remembered how Baug had appeared in her village one day, as suddenly as a spring flower, and had fallen for her quickly.

"He was courtly," said Hen, interrupting the queen.

"As befitting a troll prince," said Aghi. "The human notion that trolls are beasts is a case of the cod calling the eel fishy."

"Huh?" The troll queen lolled her tongue at her sister. "What are you talking about now? I never understand you."

"Uncle Baug must have loved you a lot, to leave his home and family," said Grigg.

"Not to mention," added Aghi, "that his power waned outside of the cave. Within, he was as clever a conjurer of troll magic as anyone in troll lore; without, he was bound by the ways and means of humankind."

The troll queen took a great gulp of the wine. Hen could smell her fish breath from across the table. "I've got it!" shouted the queen.

"What have you got?" Aghi's unseeing, all-seeing eyes shone brightly.

"I've been listening to you and thinking about the cave wall and the hollow. And it popped into my head as if Baug had put it there himself. It's the only explanation."

"What popped into your head?" Hen asked, as eager to hear news from Baug as if she were once more that fifteen-year old girl with the strange, new admirer.

The troll queen took some air through her wide nostrils and then climbed onto a rock, as if announcing some grand news to a crowd. "Baug conjured a way into the cave for his wife. He must have done so before he left us for good, even before he married."

"Yes," agreed Aghi, her misty eyes brimming with tears. "He meant to return some day."

All three trolls moved closer to Hen, studying her silky white hair, her sky blue eyes, and her impossibly short, human arms, as she spoke. "So, Baug's hollow wasn't our grave," concluded Hen. "It was the passage home, to his first family. He knew I was lonely, but I don't think he knew how to tell me."

"Baug always was a troll of few words," said Aghi, patting the top of Grigg's head.

Hen said nothing, but she bobbed her head up and down in the universal sign of understanding.

"That explains why you can pass through the wall," said the nephew.

"What do you know about that?" snorted the queen.

"More than you know."

"He does," added Aghi.

"Explain it to me," said Hen.

Grigg cleared his throat and then explained how love binds, even love between human and troll. "So, you have Baug's right to rule in this land."

"And you have the right to go home," said Aghi, "though I hope you will not."

"As queen of this realm, I should have something to say about it." The troll queen jumped down from the rock and pounded the table, for emphasis.

Hen got up and threw her arms around the queen. "You are queen of the hill, and there is no other."

**

Hen clambered up and out of the hollow with a lightness and grace due, no doubt, to goblets of fish wine, heaps of troll food, and the companionship of the dozens of trolls she had met in the depths of the cave, while, outside, winter's teeth had scraped and scoured troll hill.

She found her cottage yard dotted with spring's first blooms, yellow poppies bursting from the frigid earth, the flag that other blooms would follow. Hen entered the cottage, pushing hard against the well-sealed door, one of Baug's many gifts to his then young wife. "Heavy door, warm hearth," was what he had said. She removed her tripod pin and then the sealskin robe.

The air in the cottage was stale. Hen opened the shutters, allowing the chill air to flow freely from one side to the other.

"It's over."

The words were hers, but the meaning was muddied. Winter was over, or nearly. There was always a last blast to come. Her life with Baug was over. He would never return home from fishing, never bring in wood for the fire that Hen fed, all winter long. He would never return to answer the many questions she wanted to ask him.

Perhaps she had known all along that he held a secret, and now, at last, the mystery was laid to rest. She hoped that her daughter would visit in summer, and that she would take well the news that troll blood ran through her veins and would run through the veins of her children, too.

Hen felt strong. Soon she would take the wooden bucket to the stream to fetch water. She had enough dry wood out back to start a new fire in the hearth. And she had a new family, one that would welcome her when the summer light went out again.

Then Hen would return to over-winter inside the hill. And when she did, even the sour-faced troll queen would be glad of her company.

***

"Baug's Hollow" was published in the November 2015 issue of Bewildering Stories and was nominated for a 2015 Mariner Award. It remains available on their website in Issue 644.

In this Life and the Next

Katherine Inskip

Katherine teaches astrophysics for a living and spends her (infrequent) spare time populating the universe with worlds of her own. She is a mother to two boys, and enjoys chaos, water-fights, tree-climbing, and thwarting plans for world domination. Katherine is addicted to chocolate and Japanese logic puzzles, narrates for a variety of podcasts, and is an assistant editor for Cast of Wonders.

They tell you your daughter came within an inch of death that day. That Becka's one of the lucky ones—any closer and she wouldn't be here at all.

You wish you could hear her properly, despite knowing you can't. I'm just a silent presence in the depths of your skull, seeing and sensing everything you do. A sliver of chilled, artificial wetware, aching like desperation and itching like things unsaid.

The technician continues with his reassuring patter. But what does it matter that it's all thoroughly tested? That the HOST neuro-patterning has never been known to fail on such a close relation, that of course she's fully conscious and herself, somewhere in the crevices of your mind? That yes, there's a good chance your emotions might blur, but your thoughts are just as private as hers are?

You'd trade it all in an instant, just to know she's safe.

There, that's it. Smile at the technician!

Don't think about your daughter's body, being wheeled away to storage. Don't think about what might be years of rehab and deductibles, about how your precious girl might never be the same. Don't think of the mess she made of her life, or why she tried to end it. You're determined to make everything right again.

See?

You were always good at lying to yourself, weren't you?

***

HOST. Homologous Origin Sentience Transfer, that's what the acronym stands for—or Soul Transfer, if you're one of the more religiously inclined. The details of how it works are a closely guarded secret, but most insurers cover it, and there are plenty of online LawShops to steer you safely through the legalese. The only real decision used to be whether you chose a reputable company for the procedures, like Lifeline or Étendue-York, or went abroad for a more affordable generic treatment. It's even simpler now. They install the substrates at the paediatricians, right there in the consulting room, on the same kind of schedule as vaccinations and port integrations.

And what parent wouldn't sign their skull away as a host, on the off-chance it might save their child's life? What sibling of today would turn their back on the social programming they've been drip-fed from birth?

-I barely know he's there, the testimonials go.

-When I think of her, it's... kind of like a hug? Or like when she was small and I just used to listen to her breathe.

-You find yourself seeing the world completely differently—seeing it the way your loved one does.

-Sometimes I laugh for no reason, and then I realise it's him. He's happy, I can tell. I can't wait to hear his side of things!

-It's like... wow. I never realised she felt that way about me. I hope I never have to, but I'd totally do it for my own kids. I love you, Mom!

What most people also know --but generally choose to ignore-- are the countless caveats in the small print. That's where the grief comes in. The skills that don't quite come through unscathed. The genetic infidelities and betrayals that stop the process completely: critical mutations, vascular weaknesses, or any of a dozen other common physical flaws. And sure, a healthy mind might not be as hard to come by as it used to be, but the chemicals they use to enforce it don't take any prisoners, especially not the small, mad ones that make you you.

And even in the best of cases, there's always a chance that the graft just doesn't take.

***

I watch you in the reflections off the monitor, chasing symptoms with your eyes. There's a numb streak running down the back of your right arm, but it goes away whenever you touch it. You're craving sulphites, and your toenails throb—and that's just the physical symptoms. There are ghosts of foreign memories in your head, rapid flickers of overwhelming fright that your brain lacks the plasticity to process. But even that doesn't bother you that much.

No, it's the doubts that are the problem. The insidious question of whether I'm in here at all.

We've been looking at baby albums today. Images and vids of 'Becka's first steps', 'trip to the park', and various family gatherings that I certainly don't remember. You check the date-stamps compulsively, but none of it fits, none of it feels real.

You press your wrists hard against the table top, welcoming the solid reality of the pain. "Just give me a fucking sign, Becka!" you cry. "Is that too much to ask?"

Apparently, it is.

There are other folders further down the screen, a sanitised précis of the decades that followed. Neither of us are ready for those, not yet. You stagger from the chair, and I walk us to the bathroom, stumbling only once. It helps that you have your own idea of what we need when we get there.

We open up the medicine cabinet together, but I leave the child-proof cap to your more accustomed fingers.

***

You'd never seen Becka's shared apartment before, or met any of her friends. You don't known what to expect.

Casey opens the door, red-eyed and awkward. It's disorientating, and nothing you say comes out quite the way you mean. But she takes the hint, and talks enough for everyone while she boils the kettle for tea. You stare at the cupboard surfaces that Casey didn't think to clean, at the accumulation of splash-marks and fingerprints. Some of them are mine.

"Did she never tell you about that trip she and Shay took to Vegas?" Casey asks, before leading into a lengthy anecdote that wouldn't be my first choice for a grieving parent. Or any parent, for that matter. But to be honest, you're not really taking any of it in. You don't think you need to know how happy she was... or how broken. Don't need to question what changed. You're still convinced she'll explain it all to you herself, a few months or years from now. Right now, you're only here because you need to be... even if you don't quite know why.

"I miss her so much, you know?" Casey says, draining the dregs of her mug. "She could be irritating as hell at times, but just having her around, talking, and laughing..."

You nod. You can't actually recall the last time you talked to Becka in person.

I remember, though. I can't stop remembering. The agony of that failed attempt at dying, and every small step that took us there. We share each other's hurts, caustic and numbing all at the same time.

I push back the chair, guide you unsteadily out of the kitchenette and into the back room. The framed pictures on the wall are waiting. You lift your eyes to an image of your daughter that you'd never seen before: her and a girl that you vaguely recognise from last year's news as Shay Steffen-York. You hadn't realised she was that Shay. They're clutching each other, closer than sisters. Both are wearing identical smiles and coordinating hair above promotional monogrammed tees from Étendue-York.

Yeah, this is what we'd been avoiding up until now. What we'd lost. The girl we'd loved more than the world.

I try to blink, but you're trying to hard not to. Your eyes glaze with unshed tears, blurring the corporate message on the tees: Enjoy Yourself! - in this life AND the next!

We both laugh at the irony.

Behind us, Casey sighs. "That was a weird patch all right, after Shay's... accident. Becka was so strong though. Heartbroken, but strong. She just kinda took everything she felt and just threw it out there, you know? Nothing fazed her any more. I can't believe she actually told EY to stick it, and they still gave her compensation on top of her severance. And wow, did she know how to spend it!"

You hadn't known about any of that, and don't particularly want to hear it now. Casey's voice blurs into the background as your eyes and mind light upon the matching lanyards and passes in the photo.

"Enjoy yourself..." you murmur thoughtlessly, staring hard at the tees, and the familiar shape of the building in the background. "In this life and the next?"

I feel the chill running up your spine. I catch hard at your breath, stilling the whole world and forcing you to take stock.

You're getting closer to the truth of it now.

**

Getting inside is surprisingly easy. Companies like Étendue-York always have plenty of admin for the temporarily bereaved relatives of their employees, especially when the employee in question was last seen being escorted off the site with their personal effects in a cardboard box.

They give you a guest tag at reception, and you follow its subtle bleeps up to the second floor of the admin block. The screens lining the corridors play automatically as you walk, a continuous loop of history. The trailblazers who'd fought to make the inevitability of their deaths meaningful. Early trials, and the first glimpses of hope. The essential markers in the genes, the route that made homologous origin transfer a success. The narrative concludes just as you reach the room you've been directed to.

You go inside, sit down, and wait. It's a good ten minutes before the interior door opens: the humans in the building clearly don't run on the same smooth schedules. You sign the waiver for the standard exit interview, and agree on the terms of a sanitised job reference. You countersign Becka's original NDA, and extend EY's monopoly on her future employment in the industry by another five years. The HR drone thanks you and sends you on your way.

Outside, it's raining. You take shelter in the lee of an adjacent building, and swap your guest tag for Becka's pass. It was probably deactivated weeks ago, but at least by wearing it you won't rouse anyone's suspicions if we're seen. Then we walk purposefully across the site towards the back of a narrow-windowed lab that isn't named on any of the visitor maps.

A small flight of steps leads down to the basement fire exit. I slip the pass out from its wallet and slide it into the narrow crack between door and frame, just enough to trick the system - a technique I perfected a long time ago, in another lifetime, with a different set of hands. Next, the keypad. You close your eyes for this, the better to let my memories do their part, and the door glides smoothly aside. After that, I leave the decisions to you. There aren't that many doors to choose from, and they're all clearly named.

Eventually, you find what we came here for: the Heterogeneous Life Lab. Welcome to HeLL!, we used to quip, but the door art's been sanitised since I was last down here, and I don't think the joke even occurs to you. I wonder what else has changed, inside.

We go in together, uncertain, not expecting the lab to be empty.

And it isn't, of course. Because Becka's already there.

***

Your knees go weak. We can't decide whether to run to her, or collapse where we stand.

Your heart is pounding. My thoughts are stifled by the unheard clamour of yours.

One of us makes the choice. You're confused as fuck, but I smile and walk us closer anyway.

"Hello, Shay," says the woman wearing Becka's body. "And Becka too, I presume?"

I'd promised her, hadn't I? That I'd bring her back to us? I'd loved Becka to distraction, but I love Dr York more. What else could I do? She was mother, she was me, and I.. I'd only ever lived on sufferance. I try to express it all, my love and my loyalty, but the best I can do with your lungs and lips is a faint, lisping slur.

She smiles in a way that isn't Becka at all. It's incongruous, and it hurts. I make us smile back, pretending that it doesn't.

"You're the parent then," Dr York says, an uncharacteristic statement of the obvious. "I suppose that's something we have in common."

You stammer something that might be Becka's name in reply.

She takes a hypospray out of her pocket, and places it between us on the countertop. "Four whole months! I couldn't have asked for better results. You should be very proud of your daughter's role in the work."

"What do you mean?"

Dr York shakes her head. I wish she would tell you more, but she's smarter than that, and it's not like you need all the details of ex-familial transfer. You just need to be here. Like Becka was, for me, through all those weeks of silent, perfect, poisonous union.

It broke her, eventually.

At least it'll be over much quicker this time.

"Who are you?" you demand. "Give me my daughter back!"

"We already have," she says, then sighs wearily. "But it's never enough, is it. They always want more."

You don't understand what she means. You should, but you don't. How selfish love is. What people will do, thinking they're helping, desperate for any sense of purpose in their lives. Becka was just like you.

"Shay?" Dr York prompts. "I think it's time."

I pick up the hypo, set it to our throat, and squeeze.

* * *

We watch you wake up from behind the one-way glass, alone in your own head again. It's an efficient, streamlined process these days—it needs to be, if we're ever to achieve full uptake.

Beside your bed, a technician takes your hand. "I'm truly very sorry," he says softly. "There was a fatal problem with your daughter's graft, one we could never have foreseen."

You're weeping already. Part of you already knew... the part that's forgotten everything else, that doesn't know about the other you that's here.

I'm sorry, sorry, sorry, we echo—Becka to Shay to you to Becka again, fragments of self, fragments of someone else's immortality.

We're bleeding together now, but hard as we try, none of us can find a way out.

We watch you leave, and wish we could follow.

Instead, Dr York darkens the glass.

All the Songs the Little Birds Sing

T.D. Walker

T.D. Walker's poems and stories
have appeared in Strange Horizons,
Web Conjunctions, The Cascadia
Subduction Zone, The Future Fire, and
elsewhere. She writes about feminism,
science fiction, and freethought
at her blog Freethinking Ahead,
which is accessible from her website,
https://www.tdwalker.net. Find her
occasionally tweeting pictures of Texas
flora at @tdwalker_.

2:17 a.m.: House Sparrow—These birds generally roost at night, though some flocks may shift hours in intensely lighted environments and forage during the early morning.

A thud against her window shook Alice from sleep. Half-sleep, really. All she could manage with this deep throb in her leg. She pulled the sheet over her face and clenched her lids to try to keep out the brightness that would follow. She could hear it almost, that loud light from the street. Alice cracked her left eye to that light that screamed in through her window like a welding arc. Desmond hadn't stirred. She slipped out of bed. Her bed. Her room. Desmond snuffled. His turn next time, always his turn. But it was her window the building's owners wouldn't fix. Her window that was supposed to keep out the light all night long.

Her window.

The owners should have coated the outside with whatever it was that kept the little birds from flying into it. Little birds, always flying into windows, trying to get away from whatever was trying to catch them. Which was everything at all hours, since they kept the lights on all the time. No night meant an easier time of watching who came and went. No night meant the little birds started scavenging later and later. No night meant the hawks started hunting them down when they could.

Which meant Alice had to bang on her window to shut out the light at least twice a week.

Her window.

She looked out for a moment after her eyes adjusted. On the ledge lay the broken body of a starling. Her boss's little girl, Genesis, had pointed them out to her, told her what they were called. They came in big groups to the feeders the girl hung just outside the shop, live twittering things. This one lay still, its head too far toward its wing. A little blood and something Alice didn't want to think about smeared the window glass. Hawks got too fat, maybe they didn't eat everything they killed. She looked back at Desmond before slamming her hand against the window to knock back into place whatever circuit had broken.

Her room went dark.

Alice made her way to her bed. Her room was small and spare. The pain from her calf muscle and the blinding green afterglow slowed her. Alice felt Genesis's birding guide on the nightstand. She felt Desmond's back under the ratty sheet. Soft, warm. So unlike her thin wiry body. Big. Her bed, but he took up most of it. Careful not to wake Desmond, she slipped in next to him. He'd come to start sleeping here a few months ago. They'd said they'd take turns with the window, but Desmond never woke for anything except that internal alarm of his. Four a.m. breakfast prep to do, and him never late for it.

5:00 a.m.: American Robin—You'll find the robin a familiar sight in rooftop gardens that use earthworms as soil aerators.

The alarm woke Alice. Desmond had managed not to wake her.

He never did, pushing his big soft body out of bed so early, never needing an alarm for it. Not Alice. Not now.

Her need to run used to wake her. She dressed, then made her way down the twelve flights of stairs and out into the empty streets. She was a runner: she needed to run.

Gulf humidity settled between the buildings. Birds sang from the balconies, maybe from the rooftops too, but she couldn't hear them from here. In the glass of the buildings she ran past, she watched herself, her arms pumping, her gait that favored one leg. These miles in the morning used to be easy. She was a runner. No use trying to be a starver, like she did back in school. Hadn't bled in twenty years or so. Didn't know at forty-one if she still could. She couldn't be a starver anyway and still work on Big Mike's crew. Had to be a runner to keep up and to keep Desmond around while she could.

Pain grabbed her calf. She'd need to walk this off before she got back. Big Mike's policy: no injured workers on machinery calls. She wanted to crawl back in bed. She wanted Desmond. Her bed. Desmond with his cook's hands to knead the cramps from her leg. Desmond with his soft, warm body who could roll out of her bed and into someone else's any day now. Alice stopped.

She leaned against a window. Her reflection glared back at her, laid over the view of the lobby, filling with people. Early. Probably cleaners. Workers like her. Women in those soft blue dresses, long hair tied up just so. She ran stiff fingers through her nearly buzzed hair. Too long. Desmond had asked her to grow it longer, just a bit, but this was just laziness. She'd set the trimmers out when she got back.

***

6:30 a.m.: Great-Tailed Grackle—The grackle produces a variety of noisy calls commonly heard throughout the city. Grackles are often mistaken for crows, but the two species are not related.

Alice cleaned up, dressed in loose coveralls for the work day, and walked back down to the first floor cafeteria. By the time she made her way to the breakfast line, she'd found a way to step that didn't put so much pressure on her leg. Probably hurt the other one going around like this, but that was a problem for later. She tried not to lean so much on the tray rail.

Behind the glass, Les nodded. Les must have been what, sixty-five at least, and she still did occasional runs when Big Mike needed an expert hand at figuring out what ailed machinery twice as old as she was. Now Les mostly slung hash in the cafeteria that fed all of Big Mike's crew and those of a half-dozen other clunk operations. Clunk, what you'd think these old machines would do, but they were in better repair than most of the new stuff that really clunked and died a week after you bought it. "You ain't heard word yet?"

Alice shrugged. Les knew Alice better than anyone else. Knew about her sick momma, knew about her daddy who'd run off before her younger brother was born, knew about her younger brother who'd run off just before the border closed twenty-odd years ago. Not even Desmond knew that last one. "Run off." Not her words. Her momma's. Escaped. Knew better. Alice hadn't seen Evan since he was sixteen. He'd known himself better, always had, even though he was two years younger. He knew he needed the middle ground that was closing up with the border between Texas and the rest of the world. She did too, but she figured she could find a way. Besides, her momma didn't want her to leave. She'd told Les that one night, or maybe Les had sussed that out herself. Either way, Les knew.

"They'll find him," Les said. She slopped a ladle-full of gravy on a biscuit.

Alice took the plate. "They'll find him for enough cash, yeah," she said. Gravy seeped between the curds of scrambled eggs toward the bacon. She found a seat alone. Pain didn't make her any more talkative than she usually was. She looked down at the food. Desmond's hands all over it. Breakfast was Desmond's domain, and half of lunch. He'd be in bed again by the time she'd finished her shift. Didn't matter. She'd have this with her all day, wouldn't she? The eggs, the bacon, the sausage in the cream gravy. The way the biscuit yielded to her knife. And the thousand things he how knew to do with oranges.

A cup of coffee knocked into her plate. Petra, young as Alice was when she'd started in the business, stared at her from across the table. "You gotta teach me to eat," she said. Petra pointed to her plate. Half orange slices, half bacon. "So I can get through the morning."

"Don't think I know more than anyone else here does, Petra." Alice shoved a biscuit into her mouth.

"I see you out running." Petra wiped bacon grease on the sleeve of her coveralls, spotted with motor oil and other meals. "You gotta teach me to run."

Alice swallowed hard, the biscuit half unchewed. "Ain't nothing more than one foot, then the other. Besides, you should have learned all about that years ago. What've you been doing? Taking chances?" Can't be a starver and work here. Can't be a mother and work here.

"Look, I know I've been stupid, but I've been lucky so far." Petra smiled. Orange pulp hung between her teeth. "But Angel, he doesn't want nothing out of us until I start running, like you do."

Had Desmond been eying the younger ones? Petra had Angel, or the hope of him anyway. "If I tell you anything, you keep it to yourself, understand?" Petra nodded. Half these girls came out of what got called school now with no understanding and a lot of experience. If she taught Petra, and if Desmond and Petra did, well, no kid, no harm. Alice's thinking on that for a long time, anyway. Across the cafeteria, Genesis and Little Mike skittered into line. Their mother, Dani, followed. They'd get their food and eat at their own table with Big Mike. Happy family. Alice slumped. Yesterday, Genesis had asked her how the eggs get into the bird's' nests on their balcony. Alice told her to ask her momma. Eleven and not knowing that. What Big Mike and Dani did was their own business. But still. Petra was lucky. "You come out with me in the morning tomorrow, 5am, all ready. We'll talk then."

Petra flitted off with her empty plate and cup. Alice trudged through the rest of her breakfast, too much, more than her stomach could handle. Tomorrow, she'd run again. She'd find that middle ground. Tomorrow, she'd feel like herself again.

***

7:45 a.m.: Blue Jay—Blue jays can imitate a number of sounds, including other birds, sirens, and even the emergency action whistles you'll hear in older buildings.

"Message for you upstairs." Angel leaned against the garage door. "Make it fast. We gotta go in ten."

Upstairs, Big Mike's office. Alice nodded. The stairs loomed behind the heavy door. Just once, she'd take the passenger elevator if she could, but that'd be broken. And everyone would see if she took the freight elevator. Five flights. The food pressed against her stomach; the pain pressed out against her leg.

A row of windows, darkened, ran along one wall of Big Mike's office. No light from them, or no natural light that filtered through those almost invisible blue dots on every window in the building. Almost invisible. Against each wall leaned racks that supported the odd old tech Big Mike collected: a near-dead router and a server blinked to the dim room, all sorts of gears and shafts and half-working tools, decades old. Not that Alice could see clearly enough to know for sure what they were. Big Mike liked the old tech as much as he liked the old machines. Nostalgia, trust, something. Alice didn't ask. "Message for you," he said. He pointed to the flickering PC screen.

"Knew they'd ask for more to find him. Don't they always?"

"You ain't going to be a little pissed off about this?"

Alice shrugged. Big Mike leaned onto his desk. Everyone knew the real work, the numbers work, happened in their flat at a new machine. Dani made the numbers turn. "Don't get me wrong," Alice said. "I ain't happy about it. But Evan deserves to know about our momma dying, I guess."

"Can't send you on any special runs to cover this. Not much to be had."

"I got enough, I think. I'll just take it out of my budget for pretty work dresses."

Alice closed the door behind her. Her eyes took a moment to readjust to the bright light of the hallway. "Miss Alice, I need to show you something." Genesis held out feathers. One of them had skin and blood trailing off.

"Not now, Genesis." Alice stepped toward the stairs. They'd need her soon, Petra and Angel, the third on the Indweller run. She put her weight on her bad leg and nearly collapsed. That noise, that choking feeling.

Genesis took Alice's hand. "Are you sad?" Alice nodded. "Me, too. I wish the hawks wouldn't eat the little ones. They don't stand a chance."

"You're a good girl, you know that? Go show your daddy what you found."

Genesis squeezed Alice's hand and ran into Big Mike's office, slamming the door behind her. Alice wiped her face with her hand, then, seeing the smear of bird's blood on her palm, she wiped her face again on the oil-stained sleeve of her coveralls.

***

8:00 a.m.: European Starling—Great flocks of European starlings swarm buildings seeking foraging ground or roosts, and their whistles, squeaks, and rasps echo down the walkways for blocks.

Alice could have taken something for the pain. She should have, but the pills that worked wrecked her stomach, and the ones that didn't wreck her stomach didn't work. She needed to eat to run, and she needed to run, plain as that. She let Angel and Petra walk ahead of her. They wouldn't touch in public, like couples from higher up in the building. Or from better buildings. Angel wouldn't even look at Petra like she was a girl. So young, not knowing things. Big Mike and Dani understood, even if they didn't raise their kids that way. Alice, Lou, Petra, the half-dozen other women on the crew—they were all "hands," and needed ones at that. All living that middle ground they had to live in.

Middle ground that had started to shut off when her momma was young.

Her dying momma.

Didn't matter woman or man, Big Mike had said, he'd hire the best. Alice was one of the best of the best, or had been. She still had her brain, even if her hands were stiff. Had to be something in passing along what she knew about old machinery that ran the farms on top of the buildings. Ran the farms, fed the residents, made a lot of people rich, somehow. Pondering that took her mind off the pain, or made it worse. Alice couldn't decide which.

They turned a corner and crossed the transport tracks. "You ever think about what else there could be?" Alice asked.

Petra looked up.

"Like what?" Angel asked.

They went into the lobby of one of the large buildings. Glass elevators. Alice could look at Angel and Petra, or she could look at the lobby hurtling away from her. Not outside. Not today.

The doors opened. Alice's ears rang from the speed at which they'd gone up to this height, however high it was. Too high, but here the windows were all covered with images of blue skies above grass. Like she could walk out the window into a field.

One of the Indwellers approached them. "Angel, Al, Pete."

"Sir," Angel said. Alice let Angel speak for her. Not that any of them had much to say. The Indwellers stayed willfully ignorant of the inner workings of the old farm machines. They revered the old technology, and they wouldn't allow anything new in their fields. Alice knew that reverence, that love. Beautiful old things. The Indweller led them over to a cherry picker stuck partway up. The frame of the bucket had been repaired twice, though the rust had taken out more, and she'd have to bring her welding gear with her next time to fix it again. If she were on the next trip out here. In the meantime, she'd patch it up it as best as she could. She needed to patch it up, make it right.

"I'll go up," Petra said.

Alice shook her head. Too much to be done on the engine, the arm. "Get Angel to show you 'round the hydraulics. I'll fix this." Angel just shrugged. Alice could lean against the ladder, put all her weight against her good leg as she went about her work. Slowly, she climbed up to meet the basket. Her wrench struck her bad leg with each step. She shifted it over to the other side of her tool belt, which was already overloaded. No matter—she'd be careful.

Below, Angel and Petra leaned over the open hood of the cherry picker's truck. Like they were looking at something secret, something the Indwellers didn't want to see. Lots the Indwellers didn't want to see. Kept to themselves. Even covered over the windows, so it wasn't like they were up however many thousands of feet. The windows showed loops of days, wind through tall grass, birds flying, even rain when the irrigation valves were open. Must show stars at night, though Alice wondered if anyone was ever out to see them. Children played in the field opposite. The older girls and women would be inside the rooms to the side of the fields, cooking, cleaning, doing whatever it was they did. Only once in all the years she'd worked for Big Mike, going out to the Indwellers, did she see one of them. Alice had expected her to be startled by the men—Alice and the two other men working—but the woman only paused a moment and walked on. No matter how small your world is, you can be world weary soon enough.

"Al," Angel called up. Angel, not yet thirty, world weary as any of them.

He and Petra stood just beneath her. Petra motioned for her to come down. She leaned against the truck, resting one arm on the hood, half-smiling, the cat that caught the bird. Angel cranked the engine, which belched the smell of fried pies. The lift shuddered once, then moved with as much ease as a hundred-year-old piece of machinery could move. Alice started down, but her bad leg wouldn't take her weight. She caught herself on the next rung down. Her tools slipped from her belt. The wrench clanged hard against the hood of the truck after nailing Petra's forearm square.

Petra grabbed her arm but didn't call out. Alice climbed down. "Let me see," she said. Petra shook her head. "You're bleeding."

***

11:55 a.m.: Mourning Dove—If you want to attract these cooing birds to nest, scatter seeds on your balcony and offer hanging baskets as potential nesting sites.

They all stood outside in the shaft of noon sun that forced itself between the buildings. Petra had hidden her pain from the Indwellers, but in the open, she whimpered.

"I'm sorry."

"I saw you move your tools around." Petra unzipped her coveralls and poked at the bloody rising welt on her arm. "Could have been a lot worse. I'm lucky. You're lucky."

"Okay, we're both lucky. And I'm sorry."

Angel spat.

"You want me gone?"

143

"You're old, Alice. An old lady." He and Petra walked on, too fast for her to follow.

Alice sat on the sidewalk. Of course. Family. What Big Mike must have told Angel, the faithful little brother. Something she almost knew. The almostness of it hurt most, more than her throbbing leg. An almost life. Almost finding Evan. Almost knowing how to live here when her body was falling apart on her.

Maybe it was better if she had broken Petra's arm. No middle ground. Angel would do right by the girl. Petra couldn't stay on at the shop, but Angel would do right by her. And she'd have kids. No way to stop that, unless they were more careful that most folks could be. Big Mike would do right by Angel. Alice would have to go, though. No middle ground.

Alice walked back to the shop, the city reflecting herself back to herself. The call of birds whose names she'd never bothered to learn, the call of the trams along the transport tracks. All she'd ever wanted to learn was the old machines and how they'd worked. So she did. And now she didn't know anything else. She'd have to learn something new, something else, wouldn't she? A croak escaped her throat, the call of a hunted bird, the call of a joint on a machine nearly worn through.

***

"Upstairs," Angel said when Alice got back to the garage.

Petra sat on Angel's tool chest, her coveralls half unzipped and her hand covering her wound. "If you can get there." She banged her heels against the metal walls of the chest, one after the other, her legs swinging wildly.

Alice would face Big Mike. She'd tell him. She'd tell him

something, that she knew she'd been careless, but everyone gets careless now and again. "The office."

"Naw," Angel said. He spat onto the sidewalk. A bird landed near the spittle and investigated. "Dani needs you."

"In the kitchen," Petra said. The bulge in her cheek was more of whatever Angel had been chewing, but Petra looked like a little girl with a wad of bubblegum in her mouth.

Petra, who'd followed Alice around like a lost dog, her momma would have said. Alice watched Petra, Angel, and the others filter up the stairs on their way to lunch. After they were gone, she grabbed the key to the freight elevator and rode it up.

Dani met Alice in the kitchen with a lunch plate made up. "Eat fast," she said. "Drain's clogged, and I need you to fix it."

"Genesis making suet in the sink again?"

Dani nodded. She sat next to Alice at the small table. The kids' empty plates were stacked by the sink. Alice could hear them playing in the hall.

Something cozy about this, Dani and Alice, the short distance between them. "Sorry about your brother."

"They'll find him." Alice tried to be more polite up here, on the occasions when she'd shared a lunch or coffee with Dani, but Dani wasn't too far from Alice, really, was she?

"You thought about what you're going to do if they find him?"

Alice shook her head. "You got a plan for me?"

"Go," Dani said. She stood up and took something from one of the cabinets. "Look, it's not much, but you'll need some setup.

He's outside. Leave the Republic." Alice could tell Dani had more to say, but she wasn't going to say it. "You can open it later. There's more if you like those, ones that haven't fit me in ages. And they won't again anytime soon."

Alice left the package untouched. Dani picked at her food.

After she ate, Alice grabbed the drain tools from the pantry. The light shining into the drain was blocked by the disposal's baffle, but she could see enough to know someone had tried to destroy something that wasn't just lard for the birds in the disposal's blades. "Not sure I want them to find him, you know?"

"Sorry to hear you think that," Dani said. "And you should be too." She scraped her plate in the trash. "And if they don't, you do know that Desmond always has a good job here, don't you?"

Alice fixed the disposal and took the package up to her room. Desmond must have been in his own bed. Didn't matter. She unfolded the brown paper, which had covered three chambray dresses, each with flowers embroidered on the hems. Not cheap. Alice rewrapped the dresses as best as she could and slid them under her bed. If Desmond stayed away, if he'd moved on to someone else's room, then she'd let herself try on one, just one, and look at herself, hard, in the warped glass of the full-length mirror.

***

5:15 p.m.: Killdeer—Killdeers will drag one wing to feign injury as a means of drawing predators away from their nests.

Big Mike didn't talk to Alice about the accident, though she'd caught him once staring at her the way he did when he was deciding whether or not to buy a scrap car for parts. She knew that look. She'd been out with him dozens of times looking at scrap.

He put her on small machinery work the rest of the afternoon. Alice kept quiet.

And anyway, wasn't she itching to try on the dresses? And at the same time, wasn't she itching harder to ball them up and throw them back at Dani? Better off leaving, sure. Or if she couldn't, there was Desmond. No middle ground. Alice took a bent metal strip and straightened it. No one alive'd know what it had been originally cut for, but straightened out, it would make a good enough patch. Take it out for that cherry picker next week, maybe. Or give it to Angel and Petra to take.

"You going to break that, trying to get the crease out." Les tapped her tool chest with a socket wrench.

"Needs straightening."

"I got use for it as it is." Les held out her hand. Alice handed over the strip, which Les tossed on her tool chest. Les kept the wrench in her hand, turning the head. Its click echoed through the near-empty garage.

Alice slid off the stool. Her bad leg had fallen asleep, and the pins and needles were covering the pain at least. "Payback?" She pointed at the socket wrench. Not the open-jawed adjustable sort of wrench that Alice had dropped on Petra, but close enough.

Les shook her head. "An offer of help, more like." She set the socket wrench back in her tool chest. "You need to walk that off before anyone else sees."

Alice turned and left the garage through the open bay doors. Early evening, late enough to knock off since she wasn't out on a job, too early for dinner. Too early to go see if Desmond had made his way back to her room thinking she'd be there. Les pointed to the steps beneath Genesis's bird feeders.

"You need to figure this out, don't you?"

Alice wanted to tell Les about the dresses. Which meant she'd leave. Which meant she didn't have to live one way or another like she did here. She was too much for this place. Alice was everything, and she wanted to live that way. "Saddest thing today, you know? Not hearing about my brother, or dropping the wrench on that girl. And maybe Desmond's gone, who knows. Saw all those coming. Million miles away." Alice closed her eyes and saw it again. Made herself see it. "You ever have to pull a chick out of a garbage disposal?"

Les lowered herself on the step. "Chick?"

"I don't know. Might have been a hawk?" Alice kept standing. She leaned against the cool watching metal of the building. Feeling came back to her leg. "They nest around here?"

"Seen a raccoon taking off with a little one once," Les said. "Back when they were just starting to put up the buildings in this part of the city." She stretched her arms and legs out, as if reaching for something, some part of her body that had gone off without her. Then she folded up her arms and legs. So easy, Les made it seem, just moving, just relaxing like that. "You tell Dani?"

"What would there be to tell?"

"Dani makes an effort at least." Genesis and Little Mike careened through the garage. Big sister, little brother. How she and Evan used to play. Used to move effortlessly like that. Their voices everywhere, like birds calling through the alleyways. "She doesn't pretend."

"She doesn't have to pretend."

"You don't have to pretend, Alice."

148

"I don't." The crew started to come back to the garage, lugging tools or parts, heavy rusting things. The sameness of them, if you didn't look up close. If you didn't let yourself look up close. She'd be the one walking a little slower, arms a little weaker. Carrying less. But carrying so much more. So much.

***

9:57 p.m.: Northern Mockingbird—If you hear a familiar bird song in the middle of the night, it's probably a mockingbird singing near its nest.

The room was dark. Her room. Alice stumbled over her running shoe, pushed herself up, and felt the bed. Empty. She turned on the bedside lamp. Empty. Could be any of them, couldn't it? One of the new ones, one of the ones who'd been there longer than she had. Could be Les, for all she knew. Or Dani. No, not that. Dani wouldn't stray like that. Most women didn't, not the married ones. Not the ones who lived in the system.

Alice turned on the overhead light. She switched the window to let in the light from the streets. She opened her closet, pulled the chain. The closet light shuddered on. Her closet, filled with running shirts and shorts and shoes, filled with oily t-shirts and coveralls. Work boots. Her boots, her work. A few rusted hangers. Alice pulled one from the rail and took it to her bed. From beneath, she pulled Dani's package and unwrapped it. Who did Dani think she needed to be? Out there, the states, outside the Republic, her skills would be a bad joke. But she had them.

A knock on her door shook her from the thought. "Alice," Desmond called to her from the hallway. "I lost my key. You home, baby?"

Alice shoved the dresses under the bed. She'd find Desmond

tomorrow and give him another key. She'd find him tomorrow and tell him. She'd give the dresses back to Dani. She'd spend more money to find her brother. And tell him?

And tell him she was going to keep doing the work she knew she needed to do.

First, though, she would teach Petra how to run. How to find that middle ground.

Then Alice would run, too.

Thank You To Our Supporters

Many thanks to our patrons and supporters, especially:

Sarah Naomi Scott

Natalie Weizenbaum

Zee Spencer • Fen • Emily Anderson

Shelly Jones • Martin Cohen • Tessa N

J'nae Rae Spano • Tory Hoke

Maria Haskins • Julia Patt • GriffinFire

Want to see your name here? Become a patron!
patreon.com/lunastation

About the Cover Artist

Miranda graduated from Brigham Young University with a Bachelor of Arts in Illustration. She currently lives in Utah with her husband and two kids.

Her clients include: Abrams Kids, Tor.com, Subterranean Press, Dragonsteel Entertainment, Fireside Fiction, Crafty Games, Popshot Magazine, Diesel Apparel.

She's been featured in: Spectrum 21, 22, 23, 24, American Illustration 32, Society of Illustrations 2013 Student Competition, Nominated for a 2017 Chesley Award

You can find more of her work at:

www.mirandameeks.com

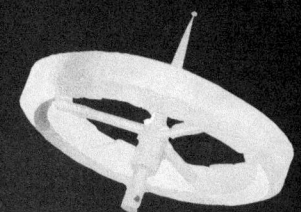